T0345574

EVERYDAY SPOOKS
KAREL MICHAL

Everyday
Spooks

Karel Michal

Translation David Short

Charles University in Prague
Karolinum Press 2008

ISBN 978-80-246-1494-6

"Spare a cigarette," said the man, and Mr Miku-lášek, a wages clerk, took a step back, this being the all too familiar war-cry of ladies of the night and those enterprising spirits that bash people over the head with rocks wrapped in handkerchiefs and steal their watches.

His caution was a little overdone, since it was early afternoon and there was nothing to fear, but Mr Mikulášek was afraid in principle.

This particular scrounger was old, of slight build, with a huge beard and very dirty, as such little old men tend to be. A cross between a deserter and a leprechaun. I say 'tend to be', rather than

'tended to be', because there have always been such little old men and they still exist. Their shoes are worse than down-at-heal and they carry a sack of uncertain contents. What drives them remains to be fully researched.

Mr Mikulášek reached into his pocket and gave the old man a cigarette. Then he felt a twinge of embarrassment and gave him another. The little old man stuck the first cigarette through his whiskers and the second in his hat, said 'Thank you, guv' then asked for a light from Mr Mikulášek's own cigarette.

"You're a real gent," was his expert appraisal. "I could put something in your way, young man."

"I don't need anything," said the wages clerk. He didn't take jobs on the side as a matter of principle. He was prison-averse and in any case felt that he lacked any business sense.

"It'll be worth your while," the little old man insisted. "It'll only cost you twenty crowns."

"Not interested," Mr Mikulášek resisted. He wasn't going to waste time with the old man. He was on his way to his favourite café, where he habitually went after work for a plate of beans. Not that he was enamoured of beans, but they were cheap and filling. Both aspects were important. As a wages clerk Mr Mikulášek was not rolling in money.

He didn't keep a mistress from the corps de ballet, which is the traditional explanation for why people are penniless, nor did he squander his pay on drink. In spite of – or maybe because of – leading a blameless life, he had no possessions. Wages clerks don't earn much. That irked Mr Mikulášek, as did many other aspects of his job. When we are young, we want to be captains, engine-drivers or chimney-sweeps; if a boy wanted to become a wages clerk they'd have him looked at by a doctor. But with adolescence the embarrassing realisation dawns that not everybody can be a chimney-sweep or engine-driver, and there's no great call for captains either.

Accordingly, Mr Mikulášek had become a wages clerk. Unfortunate maybe, but not unheard-of. He was no good at anything but clerking wages, so his die was cast. He couldn't have earned his crust by manual labour having been cack-handed from birth. In all other respects his prospects were also joyless. Once a wages clerk, always a wages clerk, except in the extreme event of becoming head of payroll if sufficiently decrepit and blameless. Mr Mikulášek hadn't reached that stage yet, and was afraid to show initiative. Any initiative in the field of payroll clerking is apt to attract the attention of the criminal law. Mr Mikulášek knew this and felt bad, because he was just an ordinary Mikulášek and in all respects undistinguished. But he was a kindly man. Which only made things worse, because everybody knew he was and so nobody was afraid of him.

Observing that even this little old man was trying to exploit him, he felt a surge of anger. He was annoyingly aware of being easy prey.

"Twenty," the old man pleaded. "You're doin' all right for yourself and you'll be helpin' a poor bloke."

"I'm not doing all right," Mr Mikulášek grew ferocious.

"And why aren't you doin' all right?"

"Because I'm no good at anything," Mr Miku-lášek said with all the distaste that beset him whenever his material conditions were up for discussion.

"Ho, ho," the little old man guffawed. "No good? Look here, I'm good at things, but what use is it? None!"

"And what can you do?" Mr Mikulášek asked out of politeness.

"Well," the little old man dropped into a whisper, "I can change into a bear. How about that!"

Mr Mikulášek took another step back and contemplated hitting the old man with his brief-case and handing him over to the man in a white coat

who must surely be somewhere nearby looking for his escaped charge.

But the little old man remained affable.

"Yeah, a bear. But it doesn't do me any good. What a waste, eh?"

"Sorry... must be going," Mr Mikulášek managed and crossed the road. The little old man toddled after him with a persistence worthy of better things.

"I say, young man, aren't you interested?"

"Oh, very interested, very," Mr Mikulášek sighed, silently praying that not all madmen were aggressive.

"You know," the old man twittered on, holding the wages clerk by the sleeve, "it's not at all difficult. In the Great War, when I was in the Bukovina..."

"Good-bye," said Mr Mikulášek.

"...one chap was about to be hanged," the bothersome ancient went on, quite unperturbed and apparently sure in the belief that Mr Mikulášek would not gnaw his sleeve off like a fox its trapped paw. "They were going to hang him. A real scruffy old bloke he was."

Mr Mikulášek sullenly noted to himself that the old boy lacked a degree of self-criticism.

"I was a corporal at the time, and a corporal... a corporal counted for somethin'," the old man went on disjointedly, "and I let him escape out the back. And he knew how to do it, I mean the bear thing. Turn into one, you know, and he taught me how to do it for lettin' him escape, the old bloke I mean. He would've done it himself, but he didn't have the right finger, he'd lost it somewhere. What you do is stick this ring on, he gave it to me," he said, pointing to the wide brass ring on his unwashed finger. "It goes on the middle finger of your right hand, then you turn it three times to the left and twice to the right. But this groove," Mr Mikulášek noted the transverse indentation cut deep into the brass, "this groove has to be turned towards your palm. It's not hard, I managed to remember it straight off. Then two turns to the left and three to the right, and things are back where they were. And if you get it wrong, you just take it off, put it back on again and start from scratch, nothin' can go wrong. But I can't show you here, there's too many people about. Try it out at home. Here you are."

The little old man grabbed Mr Mikulášek's hand, stuck the ring on his finger and scuttled off. Our payroll clerk looked, horrified, at the broad brass ring on his finger. Then he ran off after the little old man and grabbed him by his flimsy, patched overcoat. The old man turned his wrinkled face towards him and twitched his beard.

"What's up?" he muttered, "three times to the left, twice to the right, the groove towards your palm, then back again – twice left, three times right and the groove towards the back of your hand, that's all."

"Oh no," Mr Mikulášek resisted, "I can't take it from you. I don't want it. Take it back."

The little old man pushed his hand away.

"Just you keep it, sir, you 'ave it. Since you say you're not well off, you can 'ave it for nothin'. It's no use anyway, what can an old man like me do wi' it? You're young, it'll serve you well. – But give me the twenty, go on," he added quickly in case his victim had second thoughts.

He got the money. Of course he did. He secreted it in his hat. Mr Mikulášek concluded that, as madmen went, this little old man was pretty wily, and because he was no longer afraid of him he decided to make him expand on his story. With feigned trust he asked:

"What happens to clothes?"

"They become your fur, do stop worryin'."

"And if I was wearing swimming trunks?"

"Well, you'd have your summer coat. But go on now, I don't know any more than that. Try it and see. It's no use anyway, believe me. Good day to you, sir, good day and thank you very much."

That day Mr Mikulášek didn't have his beans. He was cross and wanted to avoid any further expense. He went home to his lodgings, glanced into the kitchen to check whether his landlady was in and, back in his room, put his legs up on the table. He lit a cigarette, carefully replaced the dead match back in the box and began to examine his dubious acquisition.

The ring was worn, nearly half an inch wide, and with faint traces of an inscription running round the inner rim. It wasn't in Roman lettering, and Mr Mikulášek couldn't recognise any other. His surprise at the little old man's imagination hadn't quite evaporated. He had read about werewolves, but he had no idea whether there were also were-bears. To the best of his knowledge, man's powers of reincarnation were limited to changing into a wolf. He concluded that the figments of the old man's imagination did not come from any recognised authorities.

A bear, eh, the idea vexed him. Suppose there was a were-beetle that could change into a beetle. Crazy.

He dropped the ring in a drawer, covered it with an old newspaper and began musing sorrowfully on the ease with which some people can earn twenty crowns. But after a while it got the better of him: he retrieved the ring from the drawer, looked at it with distaste, then stuck it on the middle finger of his right hand. With some uncertainty he got up and stood in front of his cracked mirror.

All of this he did with a sense of acting like an idiot, but because he was alone in the flat he didn't mind.

"Three times to the left, twice to the right," he reminded himself and turned the ring accordingly.

Then he looked in the mirror.

Staring back at him he saw his own small, yellowy-brown, malevolent eyes. He half-opened his muzzle in surprise and a trickle of saliva dripped from one corner.

"Grrrrr," he grunted in horror, took two steps back and sat down on a chair. The chair broke under his weight and he landed on the worn rug, leaving a number of deep claw-marks on the table edge.

Having survived the initial shock, he discovered that changing back into a man was a bit trickier, because the claws on his other paw kept slipping on the smooth metal of the ring. The solution was to stick his whole paw in his maw and twist the ring with his teeth.

Mr Mikulášek didn't sleep a wink that night. He rejoiced, as is only human, at having something that others didn't. However, he turned up for work at the proper time because duty was one thing, fun and games another.

Outside his office Mr Valenta was already waiting for him. The gaffer, sorry, foreman.

"This place is a shambles," he said noisily. "We work our hides off and you lot sit in your offices twiddling your thumbs."

"Do come in, Mr Valenta," the payroll clerk said politely, opening the office and letting the foreman go first. Valenta paused in the doorway. He preferred an audience when having a set-to.

"Well, are we going to get paid for the overtime or not?"

Mr Mikulášek squeezed by under his shoulder and glanced into his paperwork.

"I'm afraid not," he apologised, "no overtime was approved."

"How come?" Mr Valenta asked, hunching his neck menacingly down into his shoulders.

"That's the way things are. It wasn't approved, so it can't be paid."

"Why not?"

"I'm sorry, I don't know."

"So who the hell does?" Valenta's voice had risen

as he mellowed at the prospect of a noisy public dingdong.

"The site manager. I just do the accounts."

Such frivolous buck-passing made Valenta righteously indignant. Shouting at payroll clerks was his favourite pastime and he didn't take kindly to having it spoilt. Basically, he meant no ill, but shouting had become as vitally necessary to him as, say, daphne to goldfish. Because Mr Mikulášek was the last and only wages clerk at his mercy, he found it terribly hard to take any unsportsmanlike manoeuvre.

"So, do we get it or not?"

"Sorry," Mr Mikulášek shrugged. This meant that the interview was over and the time for work had come.

The foreman lumbered over to his desk.

"Look here, I don't give a shit for your excuses! Pay up now! All you do is try to put it on someone else, and ..."

The wages clerk took refuge behind his desk. He was used to being shouted at, but his sleepless night had left him very edgy. He was afraid he might burst into tears at any moment.

"Don't you shout at me," he said, his voice faltering.

Valenta was secretly jubilant. As we all know, the bleating of a baby goat excites a lion.

"And you don't tell me what to do! You! Pay me what I'm owed or I'll make matchwood out of this dump!"

Mr Mikulášek cowered behind his desk. He was determined that this threat should not be carried out.

"You be careful," he warned, "or..."

"Or what?" roared the foreman, thumping the table with his fist.

Mr Mikulášek felt that the foreman might devour him at any moment. Three times to the left, twice to the right, he repeated to himself mentally. "Ooaahaaaavrr," he then said out loud, pulled himself up to his full height and bared his yellowed fangs.

The foreman thrust out his arms with the gesture of a churchwarden who has suddenly espied the devil incarnate. He let out a few squawks like a terror-stricken chicken and, waving his arms in front of him, staggered back out into the corridor. Then he slammed the office door and took to his lumbering heels, screaming like a strangled hare.

Once his shrieks had died away in the distance, the wages clerk's hasty efforts to change back left his entire paw covered in saliva. He had noticed before that any excitement caused his ursine organism to over-produce the stuff, which made the job harder. He had barely sat back down, his face slightly pale, and opened up his files, when the site manager burst in.

"Good morning," Mr Mikulášek greeted him politely. The latter ignored the greeting.

"What on earth did you do to Valenta?" he asked.

"Me? To Valenta?"

"Of course you; it wasn't me. Valenta came flying into my office complaining that you'd roared at him like a bear. Then he collapsed. They've sent for an ambulance."

"I…"

"I don't want to know! I won't have it! I've got a deadline to meet and you go and bawl out one of the men fit to make him collapse. Where am I going to find another foreman, eh? Are you going to stand in for him? We'll see what management has to say about this!"

Bang, crash, wallop.

The bang and crash came as he thumped the table. The wallop was the door.

The following day, Mr Mikulášek was summoned to the management offices, where he was hauled over the coals for bullying.

"How d'you do it?" the old head of payroll asked him on the side. "Did you haul him over the coals? What did you say to him?"

"He was drunk," the clerk lied shamelessly, but he felt an unaccustomed sense of pride.

By evening, however, his pride gave way to serious reflection. He was a practical man. Turning into a bear was undoubtedly a fantastic aptitude. But facing up to being a bear was painful. Any aptitude must be fully appreciated, otherwise it affords no warmth, and Mr Mikulášek was a firm believer in appreciation on earth. Wages clerks inclined to reckon with the possibility of their temporal deeds being appreciated only in heaven usually die young. Of one thing Mr Mikulášek was certain: his ability to metamorphose into a bear could not be properly appreciated in his present profession. It was a trick, a skill, a stunt, and that could be exploited for profit.

He believed he was on the right track. He took a day off and went first thing in the morning to the Music and Arts Agency.

MAA, he pondered, that could be like a lion roaring; I bet they're all circus folk.

Human resources was housed on the ground floor of a tenement block, a fact that already struck Mr Mikulášek as inappropriate and sordid. Nowhere could he see any merry-go-round horses, or even a mermaid, and the man at the desk was another letdown: unconsciously he had been expecting a ringmaster with a brightly coloured sash round his belly. The man at the desk had no coloured sash. He didn't even have a belly. He was a doctor of laws.

"I," Mr Mikulášek began, crumpling his hat in embarrassment, "in case you're interested..."

"Tent erectors and musicians," said the man behind the desk. "Do you play anything?"

"No," said the wages clerk. "I... I can do something," he explained naively.

"Yes, and what would that be?"

"I can turn myself into a bear."

"You don't say! And how do you do that?"

"I just do. By myself. I can metamorphose."

"Here?"

"Could do. Doesn't matter where," the clerk said with pride. He was sure that the man at the desk could do nothing of the kind.

"Hm," the man at the desk rubbed his chin, "a bear. A big, brown bear?"

"That's right," the clerk agreed joyfully. "A big, brown bear."

He gazed with damp, devoted eyes at the man behind the desk who had understood him. The man behind the desk produced half a smile and started rifling in his drawer.

"Please wait outside," he wheezed. "Don't go anywhere, I'll call you back in a moment."

Mr Mikulášek knew what he meant.

"I'm not mad," he protested, "I really can do it."

"Of course you're not mad, of course not, but just wait awhile in the waiting-room, I have to make an urgent phone call. Then we can have a proper chat about things and you can give me a demonstration, then we'll bring in some other people to watch..."

"Just a minute," said Mr Mikulášek and the deadly earnestness of his expression made the lawyer let go of his heavy marble paperweight. "I'll do it for you, but don't be afraid."

He turned the ring and twisted his muzzle into an affable grin so as not to cause offence. Human resources shot under the desk like a weasel.

Shortly thereafter Mr Mikulášek was again crumpling the rim of his hat, smiling modestly. The personnel manager returned to his chair and made a good job of pretending that he had no idea what the underside of his desk looked like.

"All right," he said ruminatively. "So that much is clear. But what can you do?"

"But surely..."

"Yes, yes. I know. But what can you do as a bear?"

Mr Mikulášek stiffened.

"Please understand," the official was tapping the table with his pencil. "As a man you can change into a bear. Okay, so far, so good. But if we are to divert the public, give them something of value, you understand, not just some formal trick of the kind they could see at any old circus, you'll also have to do as a bear something that ordinary bears can't do. Dance on a ball, work out on the parallel bars or some such thing. Is there something?"

"No," Mr Mikulášek replied, depressed. He couldn't dance in the ordinary way, let alone on a ball.

"What's your day job?"

"Wages clerk."

"There's nothing there then. Animals that can count are old hat. How about balancing a bottle on your snout? Could you?"

"To tell you the truth, I've never tried."

"So you probably can't. That sort of thing takes practice, my friend, practice. The thing is, these days a modern, sophisticated audience demands high-end artistry, not the sort of cheap busking you do. Otherwise it would be the end of taste. The circus, my friend, it's not just gaping with amazement, it's the recognition of and admiration for the hard work and perseverance of our artistes, who... in short..."

The lawyer was floundering and desperately trying to remember what the circus was like when he had last seen one at the age of eight. In the end he gave up. He was alone in the room.

Outside the building, the wages clerk spat on the blue-and-white sign, took out his indelible pencil and wrote across the sign in his fairest hand: *The circus is crap.* Then he added *Ugh!* and double-underlined it meticulously, sensing that his talent would be submerged in the company of clowns.

At a supermarket he bought a jar of honey. When he got to his digs, he stood it on the floor and locked himself in. He drew the blind, sat down under the table and changed himself into a bear.

He opened the jar with his teeth, rubbed his belly with one hand as he'd seen other bears do, and tipped the jar's contents into his mouth.

The thick honey was very sluggish in oozing out of the jar. Mr Mikulášek patted its bottom. As if to spite him, the honey slopped over the edge of the jar and ran in heavy gobbets down his paws as far as his elbow, finally soiling the pale fur on his chest and belly. He let out a squeak of despair. He spent a moment trying hopelessly to lick the mess off his coat, then changed himself back and dashed to the washroom to salvage his clothes. He scraped the rest of the honey out of the jar onto a plate with a spoon, then, in bear form, carefully licked it clean. Then he turned the ring, sat down at his desk and, pencil in hand, stared long and hard at a lithograph of the poet laureate, seeking inspiration.

"Now then," said the amiable gentleman in the offices of *Science and Life*, "the taste sensations of the bear. You a physiologist?"

"Bear," the wages clerk replied absent-mindedly, as he removed some sticky spots from his lapel with a wet finger.

"Pull the other one," said the amiable editor, and patted the manuscript into a tidy pile. "Don't mind that, it'll wash off. What kind of bear? For the heading, you know. Big lips?"

"Not really," Mr Mikulášek said modestly. "Pale belly, otherwise brown."

The amiable gentleman raised an eyebrow and leafed through a few pages of the manuscript. Mr Mikulášek watched him with a sense that at that very moment time had stood still.

"Brown," he fussed helplessly, "it was very brown."

"All sorts of things are brown," said the amiable gentleman, looking over the pages of the manuscript at Mr Mikulášek. "Stop licking your clothes. Where did you see it? In the wild? In captivity?"

"How shall I put this..."

"Speak plainly. The actual words don't matter. So, where did you see it. Don't be afraid!"

Exceptionally, the wages clerk was not afraid and so replied with a whole sentence:

"I saw it in the mirror."

"That being so," the amiable gentleman said

kindly, handing him the manuscript, "that being so, it can't have been a bear. Forgive me, it's out of the question. Bears don't live in mirrors. They wouldn't have anything to eat there, see. Have a look at Brehm's work."

The world is a wicked, dismal place, Mr Mikulášek meditated on his way out – and utterly absurd. I can do something no one else can do, and either people don't believe me, or they decline to be amazed by it. I expect it's because they can't equal it, so they envy my uniqueness. But I'm not going to leave matters at that. In the past, no one was afraid of me, and now I've frightened even Valenta, so something must have changed. In the past they were stronger and I had to be afraid of them. Now they're afraid of me, so now I must be the stronger one. A bear, that's not someone to be taken lightly. The bear is master of the landscape and feared far and wide. It rips cattle to shreds, and other things.

But at this point he sensed something didn't quite fit. The capabilities of a bear and the inhibitions of a wages clerk did not make the happiest of combinations and Mr Mikulášek could not combat the idea that if he ripped a heifer to shreds as a bear, as a wages clerk he would be locked up in a padded cell. He was also slightly puzzled as to what he would do with a shredded heifer. It didn't strike him as being good to eat.

He strode the now busy streets with his head down, sunk deep in contemplation. As a side-effect of his intense mental activity, he wore a very silly grin.

Ripping cattle to shreds, he mused, is, on the one hand, pure exhibitionism, and, on the other, pretty nasty. It will get me nowhere. But I must do something. I must put my aptitudes to some use. This is the best chance I've ever had. If I don't get my ideas together, they'll be pushing me around again till the day I die.

No one had ever actually pushed him around, but despite that he worked himself into a lather with imaginings of past injustices.

Until now, everybody's treated me like dirt and I've put up with it. I never realised how exceptional I am, but now I know. I know my worth and I'll do something about it. Things can't go on like this.

What does society do? Society rejects my talent and my services; it despises them. And what shall I do? I shall go my own way.

The idea so excited him that he started skipping merrily as he walked along, getting in the way of a dustman in the performance of his duties.

"Idiot, can't you see what I'm doing?" the dustman asked bluntly, as he trundled a bin. Mr Mikulášek, immersed in his dream, was grossly offended by this intrusion.

"I am having serious thoughts," he retorted gruffly. "I couldn't care less about your bin and its contents."

The dustman grew angry and didn't mince his words. In the end he said that he would stuff the wages clerk in the bin, adding how he proposed to do it. The wages clerk took fright at the prospect. But he suddenly remembered his power. And he decided to intimidate the dustman.

"Would you stuff a bear in it as well?"

"What a bloody stupid question!" the dustman said, taken aback.

"That's what you think," Mr Mikulášek said,

smiling equivocally, and he went triumphantly on his way, leaving his opponent to his consternation.

The dustman called to one of his colleagues. They were both very puzzled and tapped their foreheads meaningfully. It was obvious to them that a bear was too big to fit in a dustbin.

Aha, said Mr Mikulášek to himself, that showed them who's boss, just what some people need. No holds barred. Gloves off. Everyone should automatically know when to give way. It's the law of nature, survival of the fittest.

Recollection of the law in any of its forms somewhat slowed his train of thought. But he soon collected himself. If you don't need to fear a dustman, you needn't fear the law. Hence he felt very strong and would never go soft again.

A strong individual makes his own laws; that's nothing new. It would be madness to be hidebound by prejudice. What is that law of theirs? Ballast, a scrap of paper and the protection of weaklings. I have one duty all my own, and that is the duty of the stronger. The duty to milk my strength. Milk, that's the very word. And there's another word: pillage, it's kind of honest and pure. – I shall do some pillaging, he decided with finality.

This thought made him very happy. He had never pillaged anything before and was looking forward to it. He assumed it would be fun. He glossed over the technicalities.

I can pillage all sorts of things. The best thing would be something small enough to carry around, but also something of value. Not gold, I'd have to sell it. Money. Of course, I'll pillage some money, lots of money. And because I am a bear of action, I'll start pillaging here and now. He who hesitates is lost.

He turned out of a side street onto the high street. He sniffed the air excitedly and then went through the revolving door into a savings bank. Inside, no one noticed him, having their backs towards him.

"Good morning," Mr Mikulášek announced and turned himself into a bear. Then he took a few steps forward. To enhance the effect he shook his head and growled to show how terrible he was.

The first shriek came from an old lady with a shopping bag who dropped her deposit book and, scared witless, crossed herself. Two or three customers pressed themselves against the walls. The cashier hid his head beneath the counter like an ostrich then poked one hand out holding a pistol. The bear gave the hand a gentle tap. The cashier dropped his gun and, in his hiding place, blew on the spot where he'd been hit and rejoiced that he was freed of the obligation to resist. To the best of his knowledge, cashiers didn't have to fight with bears.

The bear reached a paw under the grille and, with some difficulty, pulled a bundle of banknotes towards him from the cashier's desk. Then another. And another. There were no more. The bear

thought this was enough for a first attempt. He had what he wanted and could leave.

He turned away from the window. Then he stopped. Uncertainly he tossed the money from one paw to the other. For the first time in his life he experienced a gnawing envy of kangaroos. As a man he would never have got away from the scene, of that he was sure, but as a bear he had no pockets and he needed his paws for defence. He tried stuffing one bundle of notes in his maw. The money tasted awful, and anyway it prevented him putting his paw in his mouth to turn the ring with his teeth. He decided to switch back to manhood somewhere behind a pillar close to the revolving door, but then he was afraid that in reverting to being a man he might start choking with such a big bundle in his buccal cavity.

In his embarrassment he swung briefly on his hind legs. Then he crammed the other two bundles into his armpits, gave a menacing growl, as far as his full mouth allowed, and lurched through the door to the toilets. He placed the two bundles on the edge of the toilet bowl, removed the third from his maw and grabbed the ring with his teeth. It wasn't easy because, as usual when he was excited, he was salivating furiously.

Stay cool, he urged himself. – Speed and composure!

He got a grip once more. His teeth crunched against the smooth metal and the ring slipped off his wet finger into his mouth.

Outside, in the bank, a gunshot rang out. One of the customers had seized the cashier's pistol and fired into the ceiling to stiffen his resolve. The bear took fright. He wasn't used to gunfire. He knew that everything was at stake now. He placed both paws in front of his snout and spat the ring into them, using his tongue. Then he took it back into his mouth and, gripping it in his teeth, tried to poke his finger through it.

Then he heard another shot and the cashier yelling as he tussled with the alarm system and attempted to call for help. Involuntarily, the bear clapped his mouth shut and swallowed.

He felt the ring slipping unstoppably down his gullet. He was choking and spluttering. He tried to cram his paw down his throat and make himself vomit.

It didn't work.

He was overwhelmed by a wave of self-pity at the cruelty of fate. Crushed, he sat down on the lavatory bowl, dropped his head in his paws and sought to stiffen his moral fibre. He wanted to face the enemies' triumph with his head held high.

On the arrival of some men with ropes, he rose from the lavatory bowl in all his dignity, bowed sedately and held out both paws to be handcuffed. The men looked at him in some surprise. Then they tossed a net over his head.

The wages clerk endured with resignation the jerking motion of the van with its barred windows. He knew that the time was nigh when he would be tried for his crime. He intended to offer no defence, indeed the opportunity never presented itself. When the crime is so obvious, the verdict tends to be brief. The earnest men who sat on the bench wasted no time in reaching a determination.

They decreed: "brown bear" and shoved him in a cage.

He walked proudly erect and sat down unbowed on a hollow tree trunk. He only collapsed when they fixed a notice to his cage saying

DO NOT FEED!

Towards evening he set about a quarter of raw horse.

"I say, John," the head keeper said a few days later to a young postgraduate intern, "have you noticed how bears sometimes pick over their excrement? At least this one of ours..."

"Yes indeed I have," the ambitious young man responded, "and I've explained it in my mind as meaning that bears, having come out of hibernation, look for bits of undigested food in their faeces."

The bear heard this, but said nothing, because he was a bear. He took himself off into a corner of his cage, scratched some numbers in the sand with his claws and had a go at calculating his income tax.

He was waiting for his day to come.

Mr Pimpl, the caretaker, rested his back against one of the columns that lined the cloister and fumbled in his pocket for his cigarettes. All he succeeded in doing with the first three matches was snap their heads off. He did manage to strike the fourth one and light his cigarette from the side. This created what's loosely known as a pig's ear. He took a few puffs, then pulled himself together enough to pick his hat up off the floor and put it on his head, because the cloister was draughty. Otherwise he was being very, very slow to regain his composure. The impact was still quite fresh. The White Lady had passed by him not three minutes before. As he came round a corner of the cloister he saw her approaching no more than ten yards away, which barely left him time to leap towards the wall and doff his hat.

She had passed him without a word, her long gown floating behind her over the tiles, and the caretaker was lucky to catch the dignified and amiable gesture with which she responded to his greeting before disappearing behind the corner pillar.

It was her. No room for error. The moon was shining between the arches of the cloister and cast a bright luminescence on every fold of her cloak, the bundle of keys at her waist and the veil tied beneath her kindly, chalk-white face.

And it was this kindliness and amiability in her demeanour that had made Pimpl doff his hat in the first flood of emotion. It was the first time he had seen the White Lady. This was already his fifth year as caretaker at Šaratice and he knew that the White Lady was supposed to appear, but for one thing he didn't believe in her, being a convinced empiricist, and for another he had never entered the cloister on a moonlit night. But then why would he? Until recently he had lived in a cabin in the courtyard and a mere three weeks before he had moved into some newly available upstairs rooms because the damp in the cabin was more than a body could stand. Thus did he find himself in the cloister on this moonlit night, since down in the courtyard his lavatory had been right next to his living quarters and he hadn't needed to pad about the castle at night. It wasn't that he was afraid – if you don't believe in something you're obviously not going to be afraid of it, and also the White Lady didn't have a bad name – but like any respectable man he would stay in at night. He trawled the length and breadth of the castle quite enough in the daytime, when he acted as tour guide. But that evening he had gone round by the cloister so that he wouldn't have to cross the whole quadrangle to reach the little wooden hut, and that's when it had happened.

By this moment he still hadn't appreciated how lucky he had been that chance had put the apparition in his way only on his return journey. He stared nonplussed at the grey stonework of the wall opposite until his cigarette end burnt his fingers. He started, shook his head and set off back to his quarters. He found it all utterly absurd. Only ten minutes before he had been sitting upstairs in the kitchen reading the *Education Gazette*.

Originally, you see, Mr Pimpl had been a teacher. For almost ten years he had taught down in the village, and although his unfortunate name and shortness of stature had finally led him to give up teaching, he remained in close touch with the profession at least by reading the specialist press.

In the hall, he hung up his hat, went into the bedroom and woke his wife.

"I say, Mary," he began, "I've seen the White Lady."

"Sure, of course you have," his wife sought to pacify him, "now do come to bed."

She was a sensible woman. Understandably, she assumed that her husband had had one too many

in the castle restaurant, though it wasn't his habit, and her inherited common sense warned her that there are no honours to be won from arguing with a tipsy male.

"But I really did see her," Pimpl insisted, "down in the cloister."

"Of course, dear," his wife agreed pleasantly and buried her curler-decked head in the pillow, "do hurry up and get to bed, come now. You can tell me all about it in the morning."

Next morning the caretaker woke with an acute sense that something not quite right had happened the day before. Such sensations first thing in the morning are extremely unpleasant, and recalling what had actually occurred made him feel a mite worse. His wife maintained a stubborn silence over their last conversation and was so considerate as to serve him black coffee instead of white for breakfast. To her the situation was obvious. Another valuable experience handed down through her family was that serving one's husband white coffee could, in certain circumstances, lead to destruction of the home. Pimpl breakfasted in silence, then immersed himself in the historical sources that would tell him more about apparitions at Šaratice; that day the castle was closed to tourists.

He knew it all by heart, but just to make sure he wanted to check that the White Lady had been appearing at Šaratice since time immemorial, promenading on moonlit nights through the cloister between the main staircase and the former chapel. The apparition was allegedly harmless, politely acknowledged greetings and hissed and spat only if expressly insulted, though this had not been reliably attested. According to the literature, the White Lady had last been seen at Šaratice in 1869, after which date the castle had soon fallen into disrepair to be inhabited only by a drunken gamekeeper whom no one took seriously. Pimpl could still recall the gamekeeper's no less colourful successor. He himself would take guided tours round the castle as a volunteer in those days and the keeper would threaten to shoot them and make his dogs bark, but there was never any mention of apparitions. The caretaker could retrieve no other facts either in the sources or in his own recollections.

Šaratice had been reconstructed a mere five years before, which was when Pimpl had been brought in, the old keeper going into a well-earned retirement.

Pimpl settled down on a bench in the quadrangle beneath a venerable linden tree; having lit a cigarette he was thinking and expectorating. He was having a crisis. He truly was an empiricist, body and soul. One of those fanatical collectors of solid facts who are unmoved by anything that they haven't seen and experienced first-hand or that hasn't been seen and experienced by reputable authorities. Anything that he couldn't verify he viewed in part as obscurantism, in part as folklore, depending on what was at issue. But constitutionally he was not inclined to treat matters lightly anyway. Long years spent regurgitating basic facts has culminated in teachers' becoming one of two antithetical types: one which takes everything absolutely seriously, and one which cannot take anything seriously at all. Mr Pimpl belonged unreservedly to the former. In consequence he had a hard time of it, because people would laugh at him.

Those who had school-age children would snigger quietly.

The one person who did not laugh at him was his wife. At first this was because she thought it rather sad, and later merely because she had got used to it. Since she loved him she didn't have any great respect for him. Her basic assumption was that all men are a bit soft in the head, though each one differently, and she originally held that pro-pounding the truth was ultimately less risky than playing cribbage. In the course of her marriage she had admittedly discovered that the reverse was true, but since her husband exhibited no great talent for cards she confined herself to restraining him gently whenever he did too much truth-propounding and not enough bread-winning. After he became castle caretaker she began to worry less. After all, she thought, in that job he could cause less trouble. She also laid store by her local roots. In the past, whenever the vicar ranted against the godless Pimpl, the villagers would make fun of both Pimpl and the vicar, but, in the end, they just shrugged, saying that young Mary was a good girl, though she hadn't been lucky in her choice of husband, and got on with quietly rearing their pigs. For those who kept pigs were convinced that pigs kept their bodies and souls together, which the truth didn't, and no one asked the other villagers for their view.

So, Pimpl sat under his linden, spitting and shaking his head. In time he started talking to himself. He couldn't see a way out of his quandary. No White Lady could exist. Science said so. Science was what Pimpl respected above all else, but he had seen what he had seen. Only with some distaste did he finally resolve on the compromise view that he had been the victim of an optical illusion. But the sense of not being true to himself caused him a whole four weeks of anguish. Until the next full moon. His wife watched anxiously as he ate so little and thought so much and was deeply fearful of what he might do next.

On the day the next full moon came the sky was rather overcast and Pimpl was dithering in the cloister, fearful in case his experiment failed. However, after eleven o'clock a break appeared in the clouds. The full moon peeped through and shone out brightly as a white apparition strode the walkway. Pimpl stepped out from behind his pillar and from a distance of less than three yards and with considerable distaste he let fly the concentrated product of his researches into historical folklore:

"You soddin' superslut!"

A pained expression passed across the White Lady's face.

"You bog-trottin' bitch, filthy tart, you!" the castle caretaker continued resolutely, appreciating that science and necessity were right to demand that every sacrifice must be made.

An enraged hiss bounced down from the vaulting. The Lady pursed her lips with a whimper and Pimpl felt a dollop of saliva land on his face. After the white apparition disappeared round the corner, he wiped his face but felt no damp on his hand. That pleased him.

The following evening he sat down at the circular oak table in the grand hall, where the gamekeeper had been wont to throw parties for his hounds, gave his fountain pen a shake and wrote, first in rough, then as a final version, a report to the

Ministry of Culture, Ancient Monuments Department. He described what he had seen, emphasised the contradiction between what he had seen and his philosophy, and, ending with the salutation 'Peace', signed himself Henry Pimpl, administrator, Šaratice Castle. He felt that the demands of truth were satisfied. He sent the letter by recorded delivery.

The letter arrived. In due course, a commission of enquiry was despatched to Šaratice, consisting of Dr Tomeček and Dr Boukal. It was a mixed commission: Dr Tomeček was fat, Dr Boukal thin, and, to the extent that character can be summarised as simply as physique, Dr Boukal was kindly and Dr Tomeček bad-tempered. That had no effect on his appetite, because he didn't know about it. Dr Tomeček was by training a cultural historian, Dr Boukal a psychiatrist.

The pair reached Šaratice around mid-day and at once set about ploughing their respective furrows. Dr Tomeček was concerned to discover whether the apparition had its veil tied beneath its chin or fastened with a clasp, while Dr Boukal enquired whether the caretaker hadn't had some accident in childhood and whether a kilogram of copper was heavier than a kilogram of cork. Mr Pimpl answered these and all other questions satisfactorily and with due diligence even stated the specific gravity of copper, which Dr Boukal hadn't known and accordingly felt somewhat embarrassed. Dr Tomeček took notes; Dr Boukal didn't – his hands weren't free to, because he was feeling Mr Pimpl's skull.

At the end of the session the caretaker urged the commission to follow him down to the cloister and see things for themselves, because a full moon had almost risen. Dr Tomeček acquiesced. He had a sense of duty. Dr Boukal declined. He too had a sense of duty, but he was a sensible man and liked his bed.

It was a cool night. Pimpl stood guard in his greatcoat, Dr Tomeček in a blanket, because nothing of Pimpl's fitted him. Shortly before midnight the White Lady again came round a corner of the walkway. Dr Tomeček took out his notebook, while Mr Pimpl doffed his hat, because he was, after all, a little ashamed of the previous excesses occasioned by his thirst for knowledge. The White Lady replied to his greeting with a genteel nod to indicate that her previous wrath with her defamer had passed, proceeded on her regular way and disappeared.

"Did you see?" Pimpl asked. He had no sense of satisfaction. He wished neither to persuade anyone nor win them over. All he sought was confirmation of the fact.

"We'll come back to this later," Dr Tomeček replied evasively. He did not like clear responses until he had all the background.

The next day the commission departed without giving the caretaker its finding. For some reason the subject of the White Lady didn't come up on the journey back. On his return Dr Boukal wrote his opinion that, notwithstanding Pimpl's letter, he could not assert that he was either mad or stupid, then, having done his duty, he forgot about the whole thing. By contrast, Dr Tomeček wrote no report. He didn't think it wise. Instead, he loosened his tie to show that he was back from a field-trip, then sought out his section head. He knocked and went in half-stooping; you can't show too much deference.

"What have you brought me, Dr T.?"

"Well, boss," Dr Tomeček replied, "I've been to Šaratice as instructed."

"Good, good, that's excellent. And what did you find?"

"Weeeeell, that's a bit difficult."

"What d'you mean, difficult?" said his boss. "If Pimpl's mad, we'll get him treated. There's no disgrace in being mad."

"Quite right. That's what I call a humane approach," said Dr Tomeček.

"So then? What did you see, get on with it."

"If Pimpl is mad," Dr Tomeček said circumspectly, "the psychiatrist must have found out. I am not competent to make any such assertion."

The powerful man glanced at the papers on his desk.

"The psychiatrist states that Pimpl is *not* mad. But what do you think? You were there, you must have formed some impression, or didn't you?"

"The thing is," Dr Tomeček struggled, "the thing is, I was with him in the cloister that night, so... because he... wasn't it..."

"Well then, I presume you did see the White Lady since you're having such trouble getting it out."

Dr Tomeček was racked with embarrassment. He had seen what he had seen. While he thought it better not to have seen, he couldn't quite deny it. He might have been a coward, but he was also a scientist. He wished dearly that he'd thrown a sickie.

"I did see something of the kind," he admitted with some distaste.

"Something of the kind – what does that mean? Did you see the White Lady or not?"

"It looked a bit like one, but I couldn't..."

"You weren't drunk, were you?"

"I'm teetotal," Dr Tomeček stood on his dignity, sinking even further in his chief's estimation, since that man of power abhorred hypocrites. He had long been repelled by Dr Tomeček, but he hadn't sacked him because he recognised his professional qualities.

"So you weren't drunk," he mused, "and Pimpl isn't mad. And you both saw the White Lady. Wasn't the psychiatrist there with you?"

"He was in bed," Dr Tomeček disclosed and for a moment consoled himself that his superior would vent his wrath on the psychiatrist and leave him alone. But his consolation was short-lived.

"All right then," said the section head. "So I must be the one who's mad. What was it like, that thing?"

Dr Tomeček began by explaining that the apparition's apparel suggested a married woman of the seigneurial or knightly estate of the period between 1380 and 1420; he described the evidence patiently and with relish, feeling on much safer ground in his own field than in the mire of political philosophy. His boss listened to him with disgust, but patiently. After twenty minutes, by when the account had reached the detail of the hem of the apparition's cloak, he snapped, interrupting the speaker with a question:

"Yes, of course. But what do you think the whole thing was?"

This was the question that Dr Tomeček had feared most from the outset, but sensed it had to come.

"Well, as a cultural historian, I..." he attempted a defence.

"No," his boss wailed. "All I want to know is what you think it was. Was it a trick, or wasn't it a trick, or what was it?"

Dr Tomeček confessed that he didn't think it was a trick because it would have been hard to contrive for technical reasons, but he hazarded the possibility of mass hysteria. But he at once rejected this possibility himself. Even if he had been amenable to suggestion from Pimpl or someone else, he couldn't have been made to see or imagine something that the suggester himself couldn't see because the latter did not have his, Dr Tomeček's, professional qualifications. That apart, Pimpl could have not the slightest interest in any improprieties on premises in his care.

"So it did look to you like a real White Lady?"

Dr Tomeček shrugged and prudently added that it was hard to be certain since he had had no opportunity to make comparisons with similar apparitions and so it was hard to say, since throughout his practice he had not seen any other White Lady.

"But no White Lady can possibly exist," his boss lamented. "Don't you know that?"

"Of course," Dr Tomeček eagerly assured him. "Anything of the kind is utterly inadmissible."

"There you are," the section head said, satisfied. "You know full well, and yet you're here telling me such nonsense. We have to decide what next; we can't leave things as they are. What do you propose?"

Dr Tomeček rejoiced. He felt that the immediate danger was over. Lest everything were to depend on him alone, he recommended sending a wider commission of enquiry to Šaratice to make a detailed study of the whole affair and bring back flash photographs, taken on the spot and recording the objective essence of the phenomenon. However, his suggestion backfired. This was not Dr Tomeček's lucky day.

"Oh yeah," his chief was growing angry now. "That's all we need! A commission of enquiry into ghosts! For God's sake man, how do you want to investigate something that you know in advance doesn't exist? If they don't find anything, there'll be a scandal because they'll all tell us it was only logical and we should have taken a more responsible line, and if they do happen to find something that might leak out and be misrepresented, we're in trouble again. You don't want Šaratice to become a place of pilgrimage, do you? Even an enquiry will bring out all the pious old biddies from miles around. Are you crazy? Give me something else, another idea! But a sensible one!"

On the spur of the moment Dr Tomeček had no other, sensible idea. The impression of looming unpleasantness, however, prompted the thought that the whole damn' business was down to Pimpl and his thirst for knowledge; having made his bed, he should be the one to lie in it now. He adopted the expression of an uncompromising ideological warrior.

"Pimpl," he declared firmly, "speaks in his report of the apparition as something real, and that is adequate evidence of his intellectual profile. All that extra garbage about fully realising and so on is just his attempt to pull the wool over our eyes. Whatever his motives, which it is for others to deal with, it is my belief that we must approach the matter responsibly and I would maintain that anyone who is capable of instilling in others a belief in ghosts cannot, in this day and age, remain in charge of a state-owned castle. He cannot use the excuse of insanity, we've got Dr Boukal's assessment. That, I believe, makes matters quite clear."

"So you think Pimpl should be suspended?"

"If he isn't, we would be harbouring an asp in our bosom," said Dr Tomeček.

"Good. Very good. You may go."

Dr Tomeček went. He was jubilant at the favour he'd done himself by being so uncompromising and only regretted not thinking of making the point that who is not with us is against us, since in this day and age there is no room for compromise.

His superior was of the same view. If Dr Tomeček had indeed said it, he would have been only too pleased to hear it. Except he had rather different standards. People often utter or admit to the same principles, but differing standards somehow prevent them from acting in the same way. And that's no good, because then it is often difficult to say what they're really like. With some truth, Dr Boukal could be said to be kind, stupid and thin and Dr Tomeček fat, wily and bad-tempered, because that is how they were. The section head certainly shared some of these qualities, but there was no saying which ones or how many of them. On the whole he refrained from discussing the matter. People said all sorts of things about him; for example, Dr Tomeček maintained that he was an ass.

A few days later Mr Pimpl received a memo. Since he was required to travel to Prague, he had to confide in his wife. She took it bravely. Of late, she had been mentally preparing for the calamitous consequences that would surely follow in the wake of Pimpl's determined pursuit of the truth.

"Too bad. You need watching over like a child. Why go and get involved in things like that? Have you got no common sense? You haven't, I know, so don't worry about it. If the worst comes to the worst

you might get the accountant's job at the coopera-
tive. I'll ask about it while you're away."

"John Huss," Pimpl pontificated, "went to the
stake for the truth."

"John Huss!" his wife retorted. "John Huss, you
donkey, didn't have a family to provide for."

And she left it at that. Yet she watched with some
pride as her truth-loving hubby strode off in his
Sunday best towards the station, decorated with
the badges off all manner of mass-membership or-
ganisations.

In Prague he was treated with kindness. They
didn't even shout at him.

He was taken in to see the big man, given a chair and a cigarette and asked whether he liked his job. He said he did. No one doubted it. It was in his file. At the next question he conceded that it is sometimes possible to be mistaken.

"So you see. One may be mistaken, yet mean no ill by it. One has simply made a mistake, yes," the section head explained. "And that business with the apparition, or whatever it was, that was also a mistake, wasn't it?"

Mr Pimpl sat up and put his cigarette in the ashtray.

"Well what I saw," he said awkwardly, "was no mistake. I made doubly sure. I saw it with my own eyes."

"And do you think it's possible?"

"No, I don't. I even think that it's quite *im*possible. But I did see it."

"The White Lady?"

"The White Lady."

"Hmm. And what would you say if I told you that normal, healthy people can't see such things and that you ought to get treatment?"

"I will then," Pimpl said with determination, "but what I saw I'll see again if it's there, and if someone comes with me they'll see it too."

"Maybe. But you know the consequences that might ensue from such a claim? And do you insist even at the prospect of those consequences? Do you insist, or not?"

"I do," said Pimpl, and at that moment he was far from certain that the accountant's job at the co-op would be open to him. The man behind the desk paused in thought. Then he offered Pimpl another cigarette.

"Well then, you saw what you saw. I won't persuade you otherwise. But listen, have you ever seen Chuchvalec Castle?"

"Yes, I have," said Pimpl.

"And did you like it?"

"Oh yes. Beautifully preserved, huge and fully furnished. A magnificent castle."

"Indeed so," the man behind the desk nodded. "The salary there is a bit higher, and it needs somebody conscientious. Someone who understands his obligations to society. In all circumstances, you understand. I'm not rushing you, but do think carefully. Did you see the White Lady at Šaratice or not?"

Mr Pimpl put his second cigarette, unfinished, in the ashtray. He sort of felt that a cigarette was an inappropriate adjunct to critical moments in his life.

"I did," he said, almost in tears. "I did see the White Lady at Šaratice, in the cloister, I saw her, she hissed, she even spat at me, I did see her and I'll see her again. I'm sorry I saw her, I'd be feeling a lot better if I hadn't seen her, but I did and I won't deny it. If people were afraid to say what they see, there'd be no point to anything."

"All right, very good," said the man at the desk. "No point, as you say. So be it. You do know what you're saying, don't you? So go back home, get your things and pack up. You're going to be moving."

A fortnight later Mr Pimpl was nailing a picture of John Huss at the Council of Constance on the ancient wall of Chuchvalec castle. His case might have been better suited by a picture of Joan of Arc, but for one thing that didn't occur to him, and for another he didn't have one to hand.

About the same time, his replacement at Šaratice was taking round the last tour group of the day; he pointed up at the vaulting and said:

"This is the structural jewel of our castle, the former cloister, which is one of the last remnants of the original building, dating back to the end of the thirteenth century. Kindly note the early Gothic capitals and the carved foliage on the ribs, which is a stunning example of the stonemason's craft and is executed in the local sandstone. Otherwise there is said to be a fine view of these arches when the moonlight shines on and through them. I might as well tell you for your delectation that legend has it that the White Lady of Šaratice used to appear here. However, the corridor is closed for security reasons so that no one trips and hurts themselves on the worn flagstones. So we can hardly put it to the test, ho, ho, ho! Please move on towards the exit. This is where the tour ends."

"... now all that remains is to ask the management how a man with his past could have been appointed to a position where he might have access to such expensive instruments as manometers."

The reporter yawned with a sense of sacrificing himself to the common good. Stealing manometers was reprehensible. Manometers must surely be worth quite a bit, otherwise nobody would steal them. That much was clear enough to the reporter and he was glad, because otherwise he had no clear idea of what a manometer actually looked like. – Before he got it typed up it would be eleven.

He went up to his desk to empty the ashtray. Then he ducked and leapt sideways. An indefinite dark mass had thumped softly against the window pane, knocked the unlatched half of the window open and landed with a plop on the settee.

The reporter put the ashtray back, went over to the window and closed it carefully. Only a half-wit would go looking out of the window when someone was chucking things through it. Then he turned his attention to the settee. The body of a cat lay oddly twisted on the green repp fabric, its black coat shining in the light of the desk-lamp like warm, soft asphalt.

The reporter quietly hoped that the cat hadn't been dead too long. He was young and sensitive and didn't like such things. Three months previously, in response to his criticism of the goings-on in the retail trade, someone had thrown a paper-bag containing four stink-bombs through his window. As it hit the floor the bag had torn open and the stink-bombs went off. The goings-on in the retail trade must have been on a grand scale, because the stink-bombs had been chosen with such loving care that they betokened an expert.

The reporter would never have suspected that four stink-bombs could stink so much. However, his editor had said that, in their line, each new discovery was something to treasure. He also said that four stink-bombs, or even more than four stink-bombs, couldn't stop the wheel of history turning. Then he pulled an awful face.

The reporter wasn't sure if the editor hadn't been making fun of him, though he was quite sure that he shouldn't have been because he was actually supposed not to: a man of responsibility should show respect for the up-and-coming generation. He had read as much many times over, though he couldn't be sure that his editor had. That apart, the wheel of history seemed to be one thing, but a stink-bomb another, the difference being that stink-bombs stink. However, as he was contemplating a literary work on the feelings and states of mind of modern youth, he vented these unresolved problems by inserting, in his notes for it, the insight that cynicism towards another's suffering is a sign of the most profound moral degeneration. He completed his revenge that same evening with the public, if not *ad hominem*, pronouncement that there are certain principles that any decent individual holds sacred.

He pulled on an old glove, spread a newspaper out on the table and then carefully, using his fingertips, picked up the dead body by its tail. He was resolved that the very next morning he would apply to the administration of the hostel for a third-floor room looking onto the yard. He would attach the

cat as evidence that his application was warranted, and if it was turned down he would approach the council. The lives of those who serve the public are in a sense public property, so the public authorities should have a say.

The cat was black all over, with not a hint of white, and as it hung from his fingers its paws dangled limply groundwards. It couldn't have been dead long because the body wasn't yet in rigour, and its wide-open, yellow eyes in their slanting slits were as bright as in a live animal. Its bulging brow descended smoothly to its pale nose in one steady curve. It was a fairly large cat.

The reporter didn't like cats. Alive or dead. Anyone not enamoured of live cats is surely least likely to pay them much respect when dead. There is, after all, a difference between a dead cat and a dead man.

"Who chucked you in here, beast?" he asked impiously.

"You don't know," the cat said, "he didn't tell you his name."

Its position meanwhile remained unchanged and its mouth barely moved to the sound of the words. Its voice was faint. A little hoarse, but not quite how we would imagine a cat's voice.

The reporter pulled off his glove and lit a cigarette. Then he switched all the lights on, including the one out in the corridor, opening the door into the room so that as much light as possible would fall onto the table. Finally, with both hands resting on the edge of the table and his eyes up screwed up against the cigarette smoke, he leant over the motionless body.

"Definitely," he said, and he said it aloud, because we all speak out loud when unsure of ourselves. "Next thing, you'll start disappearing, beginning with the tail and ending with your grin,

so that in the end all I'll be left with will be a grin without a cat, then the March Hare and the Mad Hatter will come along and start stuffing the Dormouse into the teapot. That's what happens in books. Yeah. What I want to know is if I'm going to stay like this or if there's something to be done about it."

"You doesn't know," said the cat, "you wasn't there when it started."

The reporter experienced a need to take a hard line, to give an order – 'Hands up!', or 'Get out of that cat!', but nothing came to him.

"This isn't on," he argued, somewhat naively, "this can't be."

The cat did nothing. Said nothing. Black and still.

"Say 'sixteen'," the reporter challenged the cat.

"Sixteen," said the cat.

"Eighteen and a half."

"Eighteen and a half."

"Accumulation of capital."

"Accumulation of capital," said the cat, without batting an eyelid.

The reporter didn't know what should come next. He wasn't sure of having read it anywhere.

"Do you want some nice milk?" he asked for the sake of saying something. Without realising it, he had begun treating the cat much as he would treat another person in the same situation. He would never have offered milk to a live cat.

"You doesn't want anything," said the cat. "You is dead. Being dead, you doesn't eat."

"The dead don't speak," the reporter contended. This side of the phenomenon surprised him more than the incongruities of the cat's language.

"Allegedly," said the cat. "You doesn't know much about it."

"What d'you mean, I don't know?" the reporter was insulted, for he was proud of his knowledge.

"You doesn't know," the cat explained.

The reporter paced the room, flicking ash on the carpet. At any other time he wouldn't have done it, because the carpet was his.

Then he came back to the table.

"Now look here," he said, "it's either or. Nobody can be two things at once. Either you're a dead cat, in which case you've no business speaking, or you're a live cat and then you've even less business to, so make yourself scarce, I don't want any cats here. I'm not a cattery, I'm a Czech journalist."

"You's a dead cat," said the cat, "and you does have things to say."

"Don't you mean *you're* dead?"

"Yes," the cat acquiesced. "You's dead, which is why you doesn't eat."

"How so?"

"You doesn't know. Being dead doesn't mean being an encyclopaedia."

This was getting embarrassing. Not only was the

cat apparently dead, but it either didn't know or couldn't sort out the various forms of the verb and seemed to lack the first-person singular completely. The reporter remembered the seven primary questions an investigating officer should ask – he had read them once in some almanac – but he couldn't remember the order they went in. He knew the last question was 'Why?', but that hardly seemed to fit the bill here.

"How long have you been dead?"

"A very long time. You doesn't know exactly, you can't remember. You isn't good at guessing time."

"Can you still remember the time when you were alive?"

"Only vaguely, hardly at all."

"And why do you talk?"

"Because you's been asked questions."

The reporter was slithering towards the brink of hysteria at the imperfection of his method of interrogation.

"Just what kind of a joke is this anyway? This isn't normal, you have to admit."

"It's not a joke. You doesn't do jokes," said the cat. "You's dead."

The reporter went out into the corridor and hammered on his neighbour's door.

"Tom!"

"Can't come now, haven't got time, I'm washing my feet."

The reporter felt somewhat relieved to hear the first-person singular. The world was reverting to normal.

"Come round when you're done, but do come, I need you!"

"Then I'm going to wash my neck," the door explained. "Has someone been taken ill?"

"No, not that, I just need to see you. Can't you hurry up?"

The door replied that the hot water was down to a trickle and that it would take a while. The reporter went back to his room and picked the cat on the newspaper up in his arms. He didn't clutch it close the way we instinctively do with live cats. He

felt the dead weight in his arms. He deposited it on his glass-topped coffee-table, and because it looked inelegant he arranged the body into the natural posture of a cat recumbent. He positioned its head on its forepaws and went to his cupboard for a shot of plum brandy. That is one of the few good ways of handling things we don't fully understand.

Then he said 'Sorry' to the cat as he turned the dial on the radio next to its head.

"... and so we must attend to an issue that is of particular importance to our work at this moment: what is the most radical way possible of preventing grain-crop infections?"

The reporter reached over and turned the dial back to its original position. In his inner world grain crops were of only minimal interest. He rolled another cigarette.

"Stop growing grain crops," the cat remarked into the renewed silence.

The reporter abruptly put down the box of matches.

"What?"

"Stop growing grain crops," the cat repeated. "Don't grow any new ones and burn the old ones. That's radical."

"That's stupid, isn't it? Life without grain crops would probably be hard to live."

"The question wasn't whether one can live without grain crops, but how to prevent infections of them in the most radical way possible. The answer to that question is: don't grow any new ones and burn the old."

"Hm, I wonder...," said the reporter, slightly put out that the cat had got the better of him. He longed to prove that even its self-assurance had holes in it.

"How do they make praline chocolates."

"You doesn't know."

The reporter was jubilant. He didn't know either.

"And where did they find you?"

"On a rubbish tip. Between a clay pot and an enamel one."

"All very well, but how did you get there?"

"You was taken there by a man where you was before."

"Already dead?"

"Yes."

"And who was it? Had you done him some harm?"

"You doesn't know what his job was. He had lots of books. You didn't do him any harm, because you's dead and can't hurt anyone."

"So why did he want to get rid of you?"

"You doesn't know. And you doesn't much care either. He asked questions and you gave him the answers, like you would anyone else."

"And may I ask what those questions were?"

"By all means. You has no reason to conceal anything."

"So, what were the questions," the reporter asked, now on the brink of exploding. One time he had interviewed a hammer-thrower, but this was a mite worse even than that.

"You doesn't quite remember," the cat replied, "the full details of the questions he asked. You can honestly say that they were various."

"For God's sake!" the reporter exploded. "This can't be an animal, it's a total ass!"

"What's that you're saying?" a smallish man said with some surprise from the door; he was wearing a fluffy bath-robe. "What's going on, what did you want?"

"Come in and shut the door, Tom, and don't make any noise. The whole house needn't know. Come over to the table and have a look at this cat."

The man he addressed as Tom, a.k.a. Dr Thomas Maršálek, approached the cat and lifted its head. He pulled down its lower eyelid, looked at its iris and ran a finger over it before replacing the cat's head where it had been originally.

"You sent for me too late. She's had it!"

"I know," said the reporter, irritated. "Any idiot could see that."

"Not any idiot," the man in the bath-robe corrected him calmly, "only and exclusively an idiot professional. The opinion of an idiot layman is no good for determining death. But you really should have grabbed it while there was still time and hauled it off to the vet. I don't treat cats. They're not insured. Sling it before it starts to get high. You haven't had it long, have you? I don't remember seeing it before. Pity, it's quite a pretty one. What did it eat?"

"Nothing. That's not the point. Take a good look at it and tell me if you notice anything."

"Like what? It's dead *lege artis*, you can't ask more of a cat. Not long, just a few hours, because rigour hasn't set in. But why? Somebody poisoned her? If you know who it was, we'll do you some stomach contents tests in the morning, because that will carry most weight for the verdict of the court."

Horrified, the reporter said he wasn't seeking the verdict of the court and he certainly wasn't going let anyone stick a tube down his gullet for the sake of his stomach contents.

"Just watch this," he lifted a finger. "I'm going to show you something! – What is the number one aspiration of every young person today?" he asked, turning to the cat.

From experience, he knew that this question demanded an answer that would run to at least two columns. Then he remembered that the cat might make a fool of him by treating the question literally, so he added: "I mean, what is the main concern of young people today? In principle."

"In principle," the motionless mass on the tabletop said, "the main concern of young people is to limit the tendency to be treated as such. In the event of any other concerns we would not be talking about actual youth, but youth that is merely hypothetical."

The reporter let out a gentle groan. Tom fished half a cigarette out of his bath-robe pocket and screwed it into a cardboard holder.

"Where d'you learn that?" he enquired with interest.

"What am I supposed to have learned?"

"Talking out of your belly, to put it in laymen's terms – ventriloquism. You can have a lot of fun with that. The last time I saw it, it was a circus bloke from Trutnov, but few can match you. Though if you're thinking of going public with it, you'll have to change your routine."

The reporter had begun to go up in Tom's estimation. So far, he hadn't sought his company much, knowing that he had literary ambitions and was inclined to drone endlessly on about them during the long winter evenings.

"You've got it wrong," the reporter protested. "You ask the cat something. And look at it, not at me!"

The doctor picked up the previous reply and, squatting down next to the cat, said:

"So you think that young people might also have other concerns?"

"They might," came the reply. "But the idea that such other concerns might materialise is contingent on the idea that the main concern has been realised as a prerequisite."

The man in the bath-robe sprang back as if bitten by a snake.

"What is it? It can speak! How does it work? Where did you get it?"

"To tell you the truth," the reporter fidgeted, "someone threw it in from the street about half an hour ago. – But what's strange about that? It's good, see, a positive sign. Anyone whose work strikes a chord must be pleased to see the evidence, because... I mean, hasn't anyone ever brought you a packet of sausages?"

The doctor said nothing, because he was subjecting the cat's body to close inspection, turning it over onto one side then onto the other and, fortunately, he had missed the last question. Almost any profession seems both wonderful and lucrative to members of another. He himself had never made any secret of his belief that journalists spent their days in an alcoholic haze and were, despite their ludicrously high salaries, so inept as to be incapable of quashing, in print, and once and for all, the then widely held view that patients descended on their doctors from far and wide, riding on the back of a pig in the belief that if they didn't arrive bearing gifts, they would be left to die a wretched death in an alley somewhere, without benefit of medical attention.

"Listen here," he grumbled, "this is no ordinary cat! I mean the normal kind, going by the head and suchlike. I've seen these in Egypt, but not here. There's no pupillary reaction, its heart's not beating. Have you got a knife?"

"Come off it, I have to live here!" the reporter argued, "I don't want the place turned into a biology lab. And anyway it would hurt her."

"I just want to nick its paw. – There, did that hurt?"

"No," said the cat.

"There's no blood, look! It's as dead as a dodo. I'd like to know what sort of jiggery-pokery this is!"

He got up from his chair and mechanically stroked the thick, slightly dusty fur. The cat didn't stretch, or purr, the way cats should. It was motionless, black, dead and absurd.

"I honestly don't think it's jiggery-pokery," the reporter said sadly. "It's as you see it. It's dead but it can talk. Talking's one thing, but I... I simply can't agree with its views."

"You don't have to agree with them, the cat's not your boss. I'll take it with me, if you don't mind."

"By all means. In my work I need clariy, and living in the presence of some mechanism that confuses the senses, well, it's not on."

After the doctor had gone, carrying the cat under his arm, the reporter went back to his work. It didn't go well. The recollection of what the cat had said kept going round in his head.

Three days later, Mrs Prouza burst into the porter's lodge at the Institute, closing both doors behind her.

"Pa," she said to Mr Prouza, the porter, who was ensconced in his padded chair, picking his teeth and reading the evening paper, "Pa, Dr Maršálek's off 'is rocker!"

"We all know that," the porter reassured his wife. – "We 'ear all that stuff about education, but just look at 'em all. Education turns the brain."

"Okay, but he's so far off 'is rocker that it can't be just education. 'E's teaching a dead cat to talk."

The porter fished a shred of meat from between his teeth.

"Why should you worry? If it keeps 'im 'appy, let 'im get on with it. Was the cat rude to you? If so, I'll 'ave words with 'im."

"I didn't talk to it, he does. Keeps askin' it questions and writin' down what it says. I'm worried that cat's givin' 'im ideas. Someone ought to report it; I heard it tell 'im it's good to kill babies. 'Eard it with my own ears, I did."

"You must be wrong. No cat says that, 'cos Herod said it. But we can't let it go on. Where does 'e keep it? Upstairs? 'As 'e gone 'ome?"

"It's my belief," Dr Maršálek explained while the reporter put the kettle on, "that it can't do the I-form of verbs because it has never heard them in questions, or – and this is another possibility – as a dead creature it has no sense of existence."

"No matter. It's disgusting and a cynic."

"Yes. Rather no. It's only being logical, *jenseits von gut und böse*. A thought-computer. It's got no specific technical knowledge, but can deduce logical consequences from the facts presented."

"Where could it have got that from?"

"That's just what I don't know. It says it can't remember anything. It knows heaps of languages and replies in the same language as the question. I've even tried Yiddish. It can't tell you the rules of grammar, but it never makes mistakes except for those I-forms. I've got over fifty pages of notes. Look, here: it maintains that treating people is ineffectual. It's better to kill people than treat them because it is very difficult to produce a total cure, whereas it takes anyone only a modicum of effort to kill someone totally, which incidentally removes the risk of any further indisposition. Isn't it a little darling?"

"Come off it! You don't agree, do you?"

"Don't be silly. It's just an object."

"And have you come up with anything?"

"There's nothing left to come up with. It's got no metabolism, no circulation, nothing; it's got all its organs, so far as I can tell, but they don't work. Cuts don't heal, nor do they go septic, there's no regeneration. And I have no idea where it gets the breath from that it needs to propel through its vocal chords to produce speech. It doesn't breathe.

When it speaks, there's nothing to mist a mirror and a feather doesn't move."

"What are you going to do with it?"

"That's just it, I've no idea. I could do an autopsy on it, but that would spoil it. It wouldn't heal. And anyway, it would feel like vivisection, cutting up an animal that keeps interrupting. I've tried chloroforming it, but there's no point since it doesn't breathe. I've injected it with this and that, but there's no adsorption. I've x-rayed it. It's dead, yet it won't decompose, and it hasn't been embalmed. No earthly good to man or beast! It offers me nothing to assist my research, so to speak."

"Mr Prouza," Dr Maršálek barged into the porter's lodge the next morning, "where's that cat?"

"What cat?" the porter replied. "I'm not your cats' keeper. An' I'm no cat-napper either."

"Don't be stupid. The dead cat. The dead black cat. It was in my cupboard."

"Oh I see, a dead cat. No, don't know nothin' about that."

"Look here. Last night it was still there. It didn't leave of its own volition, because it's dead. The only person here at night is you, and I know you can pick locks. So?"

Mr Prouza was determined not to part with the cat. For the time being he didn't quite know what to do, though he had been talking to it and trying to tempt it with milk and liver since he still hoped that it had the gift of prophesy and would tell him the numbers for the next lottery draw. If he couldn't get that out of it he was bent on using torture because he badly wanted a car and a washing machine.

"Look, Mr Prouza," Dr Maršálek persisted, "that cat is research material. If it isn't found by tomorrow, I'll be obliged to call in the police."

"Just you try!" Mrs Prouza came storming in from the corridor. "Just try! You should be ashamed of yourself, getting people into trouble over an animal corpse. Call yourself educated? And I'd have you know that that cat of yours has got some very funny opinions. It obviously didn't make them up itself, 'cos animals don't have that much sense. Fine things you've been teachin' it. Pa, what was it the cat said? You know, about the workin' class?"

At the recollection the porter bristled. Porters cannot be classed as peasants or members of the intelligentsia, so they are particularly sensitive about their affiliation to the working class. Whenever Prouza saw a picture of a muscular man wielding a sledge-hammer, he had a warming sense that he too was being honoured by it.

"Yeah, that's it!" he jumped up and pulling the black cat out of the cupboard that housed the time clock, held it up by the scruff of its neck right in front of Dr Maršálek's face. The cat hung there floppily like some little thing off the gallows.

"What's a worker?" the porter bellowed at it from close quarters.

"A worker," said the cat, speaking in the measured tones of a carefully articulated standard version of the language, "is a man who gains his livelihood through manual labour."

"So," said Prouza, putting the cat on the desk, "there you 'ave it straight from its own gob."

"I'm warning you," said Dr Maršálek, "that that

did come from the gob of that cat, as you put it, not from mine. I did not coach it, therefore I am not responsible for anything it says."

"Pull the other one," Mrs Prouza butted in, "that innocent animal didn't think it up on its own. We don't want things to go hard for you, anyone can make a mistake, but the cat is ours and will stay that way. – Ain't that right?" she added, turning to her husband.

"Not quite," said the cat, assuming the role of the question's addressee. "Where ownership is concerned, permanency cannot be projected into the future."

"See," Prouza leapt up, "that's just like it! It's been trained to make people insecure."

"What's this then," growled the police sergeant, closing the door behind him. He was crammed into his winter coat and seemed at first sight to be held together by a multitude of straps.

"Oh," chorused the Prouzas, "good mornin' t'ye, sergeant."

"Morning," the sergeant replied, shaking raindrops from his cap. "I'm here about that meat. I've had a report from your management that meat for animal consumption keeps going missing. So I've come to see you, as one who knows how things work around here. I've been thinking, who could have..."

The porter scratched his head contemplatively.

"Almost anyone who has access to the meat in question," came from the table.

Prouza shielded the object on the table-top with his body and turned to his wife with a wry smile.

"You're right there, luv. But the sergeant would like to know who's particularly suspect."

"Well not exactly," said the sergeant, " but who could have..."

"'Ard to say," said Mrs Prouza. "We wouldn't want to go tellin' tales. We're honest folk, we are. It's not us takin' the meat, you can be sure o' that. We 'aven't got a dog, so who would we feed it to?"

"Well, you could eat it yourselves," the same sonorous voice intoned, "which is improbable, or you could sell it on, concealing its true origin."

The sergeant turned sharply to Dr Maršálek.

"You can't go around saying things like that! Who are you?"

"Hm hm," Dr Maršálek cleared his throat.

"The doc's a comical chap," Prouza intervened, taking his cap off and trying to stuff it in the cat's mouth. "He were only jokin', ha ha! How could I, a trade-unionist, go stealin' things?"

"Nrane-unionin hi no annannee na..." the cat nasalised stalwartly.

"'Ere," bellowed Prouza as soon as the door closed behind the policeman, and hurled the cat into the arms of the doctor. "'Ere you are, take yer damn' corpse! You've set it against us! How can you go about takin' the piss out o' honest folk?"

"With difficulty," said the cat, hanging limply across the doctor's arm. "At least not permanently."

Dr Maršálek stuffed the cat under his coat, buttoned it up to his neck and headed for the phone booth.

"I don't want the cat," he explained to the reporter once they had settled down in a coffee house. "It keeps getting me into trouble. The risk of its opinions being misconstrued is greater than any possible benefit to science."

"I don't want it either," the reporter shrugged. "I'm not keen on the way it thinks. Let's throw it in the river."

"You can't drown it. It'll swim to the bank somewhere and God knows what trouble it might cause."

"So let's incinerate it in the stove, and that will be that."

"Well," said the doctor, uncertain. "I don't think I could. You can't burn it alive, so to speak, since it can talk, and you can't kill it first because it's already dead. And when all's said and done, it *is* a phenomenon of a kind, even though I can't cope with it scientifically, and I have no right to destroy it. The best thing would be to deposit it somewhere. Do you believe in God?"

The reporter's eyes shot up.

"Me neither," the doctor went on. And I don't believe in immaculate conception or in dead cats that talk. Things I don't believe in must go together. That apart, institutions founded on the absurd ought to be the first to adopt the right attitude to the absurd. Come with me."

"We want to speak to the priest," he announced presently to the old biddy who opened the door to them. She led them down a cold corridor.

"What have you brought me, gentlemen?" the little old priest asked them with some distrust, wiping away the crumbs of his tea with his handkerchief.

"The thing is, reverend, we have a rather unusual request."

"Be sure that I will do all in my modest power to help you. Do please sit down," the clergyman pointed to two worn plush armchairs. "Just as long it is nothing illegal. You realise..."

"Absolutely. Our problem is: we've got something that we would like to place in your safekeeping because we have reached the conclusion that you are the best person to look after this kind of thing. Unless you decline to help us, that is."

"But yes, of course," the priest nodded his fluffy head in some fright, "that is,... But what is it, if you don't mind my asking?"

"Just a minute." It was Dr Maršálek who spoke as he removed the cat from inside his coat and placed it on the crocheted mat on the table. Then he arranged it elegantly and stepped away to admire his work from further back.

"We've brought you a cat."

The priest touched the cat. Then he reddened all the way down to his dog-collar.

"How dare you!" he blustered. "If you think the times we live in allow you to do such... I don't know what to call it... in short, take your animal away at once or I shall be obliged to summon the protection of the forces of the law."

"Please don't be angry," Dr Maršálek sought to calm him down. "The cat's dead. I'm a doctor, I know these things."

"I should hope so," the old man fulminated. "What's all this about?"

"We're coming to that. This cat is dead and by its own testimony it's been dead for quite some time. Except it isn't decomposing and what's more it talks."

"Can't say I've noticed!" snapped the clergyman.

"So ask it something!"

"I'm not here for you to make fun of, sir!"

"All right, I'll ask it something. Listen," he leaned over the cat, "we don't want you, so we're handing you over to the priest here. Do you know what a priest is?"

"A priest is a man," the cat replied, "who gains his livelihood by trying to convince others to believe in something which they cannot believe in of themselves. Part of this belief is providing the priest with a living."

"See," said the reporter with some malice to the thunderstruck priest, "totally logical."

"Forgive me, I don't understand. What do you want from me?"

"Up to a point the cat has explained that itself. You are simply predisposed by your calling to believe in things that are otherwise barely believable. No offence meant. And in a way this cat is one of those things. So if you would be so kind as to take charge of it. It's nothing to do with us."

"Aha, I see. Yes. But out of the blue like this... I ought to... The thing is, in case you don't know, animals are not possessed of a soul. That is the Church's teaching. And as a priest I... I mean, I'm sorry, how come the cat talks? Is it some kind of scientific hoax?"

"Neither a hoax, nor scientific. It just talks. And it's apt to say some pretty weird things."

"Aha. All very well, but as far as we know, animals don't usually speak. It's not customary. Least of all dead ones. Of course there's always the possibility that the devil... but I've never come across it before. And I've been parish priest here for forty years. Unless – but this is for the Church alone to decide – unless we are witnessing a miracle."

"Do please witness it for yourself. Would you care to ask it something? To make sure?"

"All right then," the priest agreed, approaching the cat cautiously. "Can you hear me, creature?"

"Yes, you can."

"That's just its funny way with verbs," the reporter hurriedly intervened, lest the priest get angry again at being made fun of by the cat.

"Are you from God, or from the devil?"

"You comes from cats. Your father was a tomcat, your mother a she-cat. But people often give animals names."

"Just so, that's right. If you are an immortal soul, are you a believer?"

"You is dead and the dead cannot believe. Incidentally, you doesn't understand the first half of the question."

"It's... That'll be right. Dead, yes of course. But listen, what comes after death?"

"Death is only itself."

The priest shook his head and jabbed the cat with his finger.

"I say, gentlemen, and... and is the cat yours?"

"Yes, sort of... I got it as a present," the reporter admitted.

"A present. I see. I understand. Except, before I offer it shelter... forgive me, what is the animal's attitude to government policy?"

"None," replied the cat off its own bat. "You's dead. You can't have an attitude to anything."

"Most praiseworthy," the confused cleric smiled sweetly, forgetting that he wasn't in the confessional. Then he checked himself.

"That is," he corrected himself, "how am I to understand that?"

"You isn't interested," the cat said. "You isn't interested in anything and therefore you isn't interested in government policy. You doesn't need food for your existence."

"Oh yes I do," the priest protested spontaneously, this time forgetting, under the burden of the supernatural, about the dead cat's grammatical peculiarity.

A deathly hush reigned.

"Gentlemen, you must understand," – he crossed back and forth across the room – "this needs thinking about, so to say. The Church teaches that we should afford protection to God's creatures, that's true, and it also enjoins us to give the dead a Christian burial. But as I see it, this is not a creature of God because, for all that it talks, it does not acknowledge God by its mouth. So the best that I can do is attempt to exorcise it. But in all honesty, would you insist on that?"

"Oh no," Dr Maršálek reassured the priest. "Please deal with it as you see fit. We have brought it to you and you can keep it."

"But you see, that's the very thing I cannot do for you. You must understand that a dead cat – and you, like the cat itself, insist that it *is* dead – cannot join my flock. Care for its soul is not one of the duties of my office. And anyway, even if it were alive, that would change nothing. The cat says all sorts of things with which I cannot agree as a priest and to which I ought not to listen as a citizen."

The doctor and the reporter sensed that things were not exactly going to plan.

"So you don't want it?"

"I am truly sorry, gentlemen, why should I of all people want it? What would I do with it here? We live in difficult times. If you'll take my advice, I would place it in an animal refuge. Or, if you require a decision from the Church authorities, take the cat to the consistory. I'm too old and, God forgive me, all I crave is peace and quiet. Apart from that I've got trouble with my gall bladder so I cannot afford to undermine my health with supernatural phenomena."

"See," the reporter was reproachful, after the old dear closed the vicarage gate behind them. "That was pointless. They don't want it either. It does not acknowledge God by its mouth."

"Small wonder," growled the doctor in irritation. "Reverend father, I've brought you a goose, that would be okay. But a dead cat?"

"I'm not going to the consistory," the reporter declared, in case there were any doubt.

"But we have to take it somewhere."

"And I'm not taking it anywhere else either," said the reporter. "The cat won't watch its tongue. It must be destroyed immediately."

He walked over to the railing on the bridge and, leaning out over the water, swung the cat by its tail.

"We can't destroy it," the doctor resisted and deftly caught the cat by the head to prevent the worst. "You've no right to destroy a thing when you don't know how it's created."

"I wash my hands of the matter," the reporter warned, winding the cat's tail round his finger with some distaste. "It'll be down to you."

"It won't though. I don't identify with it, but I won't let it be destroyed. Understand, it simply can't say anything other than what it does say because it's dead. It's not its fault. It isn't alive enough for us and we aren't dead enough for it, that's all there is to it."

"Let me tell you, Thomas, I don't propose to commit suicide physically or existentially just to get closer to it. What do you want to try next?"

"That's obvious. We have to find someone or something with as many points of contact with it as possible. Something ideologically rigid, and so dead. We're too alive, which is why we're no good with it. I've had an idea that might work."

"Maybe," said the reporter and then took fright. The prospect of all those institutions and institutes where the righteous Dr Maršálek might seek attributes fit to neutralise the lamentable candour of this feline, and all the ramblings that the dead animal might trot out there, alarmed him somewhat.

The reporter was a practical man. He had no urge to save mankind, let alone a cat. He made his excuses and fled.

Dr Maršálek sat on the bridge rail and stroked the cat's jet-black fur, sunk in thought. He took the dead animal's round head in both hands and gazed into its motionless yellow eyes.

"Tell me, you wretched beast, what is wrong here?"

"Nothing," said the cat. "Nothing can be wrong. Only the ending of a life is ineluctable, sooner or later. No amount of trying, or even not trying, can change anything. But trying takes more effort."

He stuffed the cat under his coat and set off across the bridge. He whistled as he went and rejoiced as only the just can rejoice.

The abbot was sitting on the monastery terrace, squinting against the setting sun. A young monk bowed his head respectfully and hid his face in the folds of his orange vestment.

"Holy father," he whispered, shuffling respectfully in his slippers.

"Speak, holy brother," said the abbot, without shifting his position.

"Holy father," the monk said, "your wisdom shall be our guide. At the gate there is a messenger who has brought a strange gift from the land of the devils."

"Many are the things that are strange when one is young. What is the nature of the gift?"

"A dead cat, holy father. We know not what to do."

"Take the cat to the kitchen, holy brother. In humility shall we convert its body into food, for we bear no blame for its death."

"Holy father," the monk hesitated, "the cat arrived in a package bearing the writing of devils. The package is torn, but the cat itself is undamaged and out of its mouth come words in our tongue. The meaning of the answers to the questions that the other brothers and I put to it sows confusion in our souls and puts words of awe into our mouths. Holy father, the cat says..."

With a slow, tired gesture the abbot raised one arm in its flowing sleeve.

"Holy brother," he said kindly, "it is not good to squander the time that flows onwards towards other ends by idly meditating on the words of a dead animal. We may not consume its body, lest we prevent it from saying that which it is desirous of saying. But go and take the cat to the boxroom where we store broken prayer mills and rattles that have lost their rattle. Holy brother, with all due respect to your wisdom, how can a man begotten by a man who was in turn the son of a man, again I say, how can such a man be interested in something that comes out of the mind and mouth of a dead cat?"

AN EXTRAORDINARY OCCURRENCE

Major Mikys was sitting in his office, studying the plan for the forthcoming exercise. The corner of the room was occupied by his second-in-command, Captain Šamaj, who was picking his nose with relish. Šamaj was much given to concentrated nose-picking and had the habit of saying, while so engaged: "So many things to do." The Slovaks in the company had nicknamed him Gluepot. Šamaj did not take kindly to the name. At first he wanted to have all the Slovaks locked up, but Mikys had dissuaded him, lest it look like national oppression. After all, the Minister of Defence had stated un-equivocally that no such thing could be tolerated in the army.

Major Mikys rolled the plan of the exercise into a tube and began looking through it, telescope-

wise, at the various objects in his office. It was fun, and Major Mikys concluded that life was really quite nice.

His optical instrument lighted on a little ant crawling at a leisurely rate across the floor. He squatted down and inspected the ant with some distaste. Ants have no place in barracks.

Suddenly a yelp came from the corridor followed by the pounding of hob-nailed boots. The office door flung wide to admit the company orderly. His head was bare and plainly playing temporary host to the man's eyes. Mykis realised it was too late to pretend to be engaged in more officer-like activities and so blew his top.

"Never heard of knocking first?" he bellowed. The orderly stuttered something and pointed out

to the corridor. Major Mikys rose from his chair. "Out!" he said dryly.

Seeing that he was being evicted from the room, the orderly curled up between a cupboard and the crate containing all the most top-secret papers and started emitting sounds suggestive of utter terror.

Major Mikys had always believed that the men were all idiots. Anyone who had not been to a military academy could be guaranteed to lack sophistication. But this really was a bit much.

"What's the matter?" he asked in disgust.

"Out there," the orderly explained in Slovak.

Mikys shook his head in mystification, straightened his Sam Browne and went out into the corridor. There stood a ghost. It was semi-transparent and extraordinarily unprepossessing. Two protruding green eyes shone out of its hollow features, its face overhung by a shock of lank, colourless hair. Spotting Major Mikys, it tendered a long-fingered paw and emitted a drawling whine.

Major Mikys was shocked at the ghost's ugliness. He had never seen such an ugly ghost, though during his time with the army there had been a plentiful supply of other ugly things for him to see.

"Stop messin' about," he said somewhat uncertainly.

"Ooooooooo," said the ghost, grinning with its purple lips.

Major Mykis began to think someone was having him on and was about to take steps accordingly. But then he noticed that the ghost's legs ended in a kind of fuzzy haze about three inches above the floor. That gave him pause. He concluded that the line he had taken up to now was not the right one. Since the ghost's presence on the base was obviously illegal, he should have shouted three times: 'Halt, who goes there?' and then fired his weapon in its direction. But Major Mykis was no slouch and knew how to put things right.

"Halt, who goes there?" his voice rang out.

"Ooooooooo," said the ghost.

Major Mykis remembered that he would have to go back inside his office to collect his weapon, which wasn't loaded anyway, and so the ghost might disappear before he could fetch it. So he stuck out his chest and took a step towards it. The ghost whined and shook its ugly paws like a dog begging for a lump of sugar.

"What are you doing," Mykis asked.

"Haunting," the ghost replied in a voice like the wind howling through the beams of a gallows-tree. "Any idiot can see that."

Major Mikys appreciated that his authority might be dented by any such comparison.

"Stand to attention!" he barked ferociously.

The ghost failed to respond, merely fluttering like a candle flame. Mykis decided to try persuasion.

"I'm not afraid of you," he said.

"I couldn't care less, ooooooooo bla bla bla blah," the ghost retorted, its eyes glazing over.

Major Mikys took offence at such indifference. So he decided not to demean himself any further, turned on his heal and went off back to his office. There he found Captain Šamaj hard at work: he was endeavouring to explain to the company orderly that whenever he entered a room where officers were present, he should stand to attention, and Captain

Šamaj himself was demonstrating how standing to attention should be done properly. The orderly's terror was beginning to dissipate to be replaced by amusement as he watched the captain's antics.

Major Mikys first meant to order the orderly out so that he could speak to Šamaj undisturbed, but then he thought twice about it, realising that the orderly's fear of the ghost would probably prevent him from obeying.

"Hey, Šamaj," he said to his second-in-command, "there's a ghost in the corridor."

Captain Šamaj performed the response to the order 'At ease'.

"What?" he asked.

"A ghost," said Mikys.

"Where?"

"In the corridor, out there – "

"What kind of ghost?"

"Ugly as sin, go and have a look!"

"Don't be daft," Captain Šamaj replied, "there's no such thing as ghosts."

"What do you mean, no such thing," said Mikys, offended, since he couldn't bear to have his judgement called into question in the presence of subordinates. "I've spoken to it!"

"And what did it tell you?" Šamaj enquired.

Major Mikys was not entirely certain that he could reproduce the ghost's words accurately, and he retained an impression that they had not been entirely to his credit. So he left the question unanswered. Captain Šamaj thought that that was the end of the matter.

"You can go," he said to the orderly. But the orderly recalled the utter horror of being alone in the corridor with a ghost and started shaking like a leaf.

"Wait, don't send him out," Mikys spoke up to help the poor man. "I'm telling you, there's a ghost out there!"

"What?" Šamaj asked, suddenly alert.

"A ghost," Mikys explained, "a spirit, a spook. You know, a ghost," he sought to be precise.

"And what's it doing there?" Šamaj was interested to know.

"Haunting," Mikys replied, echoing the ghost's own explanation.

Captain Šamaj frowned.

"I see," he said helplessly, "so what are we going to do about it?"

This question evidently called for a decision that would carry authority.

"Let's speak to him," Mikys decided at last and went back out into the corridor with his deputy in tow. The ghost, seeing them coming, gave a weary squeak. Mikys took the initiative since he was concerned that the ghost might be irritated by Šamaj's intellectual inflexibility.

"Why are you haunting?" he asked.

"Because I have to," the ghost wheezed horribly, "or did you suppose I do it for fun?"

This question was not an easy one to answer and the conversation seemed to have reached an impasse. However, the situation was retrieved, quite unexpectedly, by Captain Šamaj:

"And why are you haunting here?"

"Here," the ghost conceded with indifference, "here and in the latrines."

"And why the latrines?" Major Mikys enquired, taking offence; the latrines were the company's pride and joy.

"Because that's where I hanged myself," the ghost replied, and the recollection of that gloomy event moved it to renewed moaning.

Major Mikys quaked. Not at the ghost, but at the thought of having to account for such an extraordinary occurrence as a suicide on his company's patch.

"Oh God, when?" he squeaked faintly.

"A hundred years ago," the ghost replied.

This answer restored Mikys's composure. He had not been company commander at the time.

"And you've been haunting ever since?" he wanted to know.

"Only sometimes," came the reassuring reply.

At this point Captain Šamaj put his oar in, being of the view that it was time to go home. However, leaving a ghost unsupervised was out of the question. So, adopting a businesslike tone, he asked:

"Are you going to be haunting much longer today?"

"Just a while longer," said the ghost. It gave a few moans, quivered, then uttered one last long groan from the heart, stuck out its tongue and disappeared in the doorway to the latrines.

It had gone. Major Mikys did his last rounds, replaced the orderly, who had had a nervous breakdown and was in the sick-bay, and left the barracks with his second-in-command. They proceeded in silence and in silence sat down at a table in the pub. Captain Šamaj downed a beer, while Major Mikys downed a brandy, because he was agitated, then undid his collar, a thing he never did.

"Christ," said Captain Šamaj after a time.

"Christ what?" said Major Mikys, hitting the nail on the head.

As usual, Captain Šamaj didn't know and gazed idly at the index finger of his right hand.

"Ugh," Major Mykis rebuked him and Captain Šamaj placed both hands neatly on the table-cloth. The silence dragged on. After a while Major Mykis came up with the idea of using the ghost as a training aid, ideally as a dummy for hand-to-hand fighting. But Captain Šamaj disagreed.

"All it cares about is haunting, probably wouldn't be interested at all in training. The best thing would be to seal the latrines and stop worrying."

Major Mikys objected vigorously. He laid great store by the latrines in the context of the forthcoming inspection. His misery was compounded by Captain Šamaj's next remark:

"The ghost will have to be reported upstairs. A ghost is an extraordinary occurrence, and you won't persuade me otherwise."

"Oh, God," Major Mykis groaned.

"Yep," said Captain Šamaj, "needs explaining. Why, and all that."

Major Mykis ordered another brandy.

"Of course, it might not come back," his second-in-command sought to reassure him.

"But what if it does," his chief voiced his misgivings. They both knew how bad that would be. They were very sad and sorry for themselves, because they were afraid.

"I know, Šamaj," Major Mikys suddenly yelped gleefully. "I've got it! Listen to this; it's a great idea. Let's pretend it doesn't exist."

"What d'you mean?" Šamaj didn't understand – he'd just been turning over in his mind the topography of the remotest military postings with special reference to the deployment of particularly obnoxious garrisons.

"Just that. We'll simply pretend it doesn't exist and that nobody has seen it. Normal people don't see ghosts because there aren't any. It makes sense, doesn't it?"

"Okay," said Šamaj uncertainly, "but what if someone does see it?"

"Anyone who sees it will be punished," Major

Mikys said resolutely and did up his collar. "For spreading alarm and undermining morale. Understood? – The bill, please."

"Punished," Captain Šamaj's spirits rose, this being an area in which he felt at home. "There are no ghosts," he declared with glorious self-assurance, "we can't be doing with ghosts; so many things to do – and a ghost on top of everything!"

And at the mention of things to do his finger crept surreptitiously back towards his nose.

THE COCKABOGEY

Mr Houska, a paviour, got drunk on Tuesday. This was somewhat out of the ordinary, since like any decent man he usually didn't get drunk until Saturday, but that Tuesday it was raining, so he had no option. At first the rain had been quite gentle, but then it started to pour down; by chucking-out time, ten thirty, there was a fine, dense and persistent drizzle. Houska aimed a few kicks at the drawn roller-shutter of the King's Head, whence he had been ejected. Having thus asserted his moral superiority over all publicans, he turned up his collar and strode off towards home. The street lamps flickered into the wet night and water gurgled down from gutters, trees and roofs. As he pushed the key into his front door he caught sight of an egg lying under the drainpipe. It was a white egg, with black speckling, and it glistened under the trickle of water that was falling straight onto it. Quite an ordinary egg, slightly pointed at one end, a bit larger than a hen's. Houska the paviour picked it up and popped it in his pocket because, unlike hens, he believed eggs were for eating.

Once indoors he cursed roundly for a time, having barked his shin on the washtub, then lay down to sleep without undressing. He sensed that the slightest effort would cause him to throw up.

In the morning he got up tormented by an acute thirst. On the duvet he noticed some fragments of white, black-speckled eggshell. He recollected the egg that he had picked up the night before from under the drainpipe and which he must have squashed in the night, so he half-lifted the duvet in search of its contents. Underneath the duvet sat a black chicken, an ugly chicken with a long neck and green eyes, huddled shivering in a corner of the bed.

What little Houska knew about the consequences of long-term intemperance was sufficient for him to withdraw into a corner and let out a strangulated roar. As he fought a relentless inner struggle in order to demonstrate that he could take his delirium like a man, the chicken hopped out of the bed, hurting itself slightly, and, hobbling on its gangly legs, headed for the door, where Houska had some socks soaking in a basin. It took a long sip, coughed, stretched and flapped its wings, on which feathers had begun to sprout.

In his corner, Houska the paviour was beginning to gain some mastery over the situation.

"Clucky-clucky-clucky," he experimented. The chicken looked him up and down with a sidelong look of its green eyes.

"Don't be soppy," it said ironically. "Crumble me some bread, I'm hungry."

Houska's second roar ended in a groan.

"Oh no, oh no," Houska whined, "I'm going mad, I can't take this!"

"Cut that out," said the chicken, getting fed up. "I can't take this first thing in the morning. Get me some bread and stop gawping. You've got to feed me now you've hatched me."

"How so?" came from the corner.

"Under your backside, my friend, under your backside," the chicken declared dryly. "I'm not a chicken, I'm Cockabogey. And hurry up with that bread, we're off to work!"

Houska wasn't clear what Cockabogey was. He concluded that it was some creature that chased people to work, so he started to think of a way to put it down. Meanwhile he was afraid of it, so he brought it some bread and left the house with Cockabogey at his heels. On the way Cockabogey maintained a tactful silence, and Houska didn't feel much like talking either.

The lights at the crossroads were at red. Houska stopped, but Cockabogey wove in and out of the traffic and waited on the other side. The traffic policeman popped out of his box and went up to Houska.

"In case you didn't know, poultry must not roam free in built-up areas, but must be carried in a basket or by the feet. Don't go forgetting that or you'll be in for a fine."

Once across the road, Houska took Cockabogey under his arm, being afraid to carry it by its feet. Cockabogey promptly pecked his ear.

"You stink," it declared. "Put me down and get a move on or we'll be late!"

When they got to his work-site, Houska knuckled down at a spot far away from the others, being embarrassed because of Cockabogey. The latter squatted on a fence and watched Houska as he worked.

"What's that you're doing?" it asked after a while.

"Mosaic paving," Houska explained. "First you have to spread out some sand and lime, then you set one of these stones in it, black or red, you scrape out a hole, tap the stone in, then on to the next one.

When it's all done, you scatter lime on it, sprinkle it with water and go over it with a brush."

"Is that all?" asked Cockabogey with a sneer.

"Yeah," Houska conceded, "but it has to be level."

Cockabogey hopped down from the fence.

"Out of the way," it said. It picked a stone from the pile with its beak, scraped a hole in the sand with its claw, positioned the stone and hammered at it with its yellow beak like a cobbler at a sole. Then it spun round on the stone with its bare rump to make sure it was sitting level and scuttled off for another.

If Houska had still been capable of surprise at anything, he would surely have been amazed at how a chicken, so weak at first sight, could work wonders with mosaic paving. Five metres were ready in no time.

"Wheelbarrow," Cockabogey bellowed. "Bring me lime, sand, stones! So I don't have so far to run!"

Houska bent obediently for the barrow while

Cockabogey ran up and down the finished work and tapped down any projecting stones.

"You can do the watering yourself," it shouted, "it's slowing me down."

As soon as Houska hurried off for a fresh can of water, Cockabogey started whirling round on its rump and wings and spreading the grout evenly.

By ten o'clock Houska was feeling hot. Being utterly in thrall to Cockabogey by now, he asked if he might go for a beer.

"No beer!" Cockabogey objected. "There's work to be done, so we do it. And add more lime, this is all sand!"

Houska took a melancholy drink from the watering can.

At eleven o'clock the supervisor arrived on his motor-bike. When Cockabogey saw him, it hopped onto the fence and started picking dry grout out of its claws. The supervisor paid it no attention and made a rough estimate of the work done.

"That's all today's?" he asked Houska.

"Yes."

"And how long have you been at it?"

"Since six."

"Not before? And you've done all this? Pull the other one!" he declared, got back on his motor-bike and rode off.

"Barrow!" squawked Cockabogey and hopped down from the fence.

At two o'clock it allowed Houska to call it a day. Back home, Houska flopped onto his bed, worn out by work, the morning's hangover and the lack of beer. First he had to crumble some bread for Cockabogey, who then had a drink of sock-water and hopped lightly about the room.

"How much did we make today?" it asked. Houska totted it up in his head.

"Two hundred and sixty crowns."

Cockabogey refrained from comment.

The next day it was three hundred and twenty. The supervisor gave Houska a rocketing.

"You all think I don't know anything," he hollered. "But I do. Old Pozner is on twelve hundred invalidity benefit, but he's so greedy he comes here early and helps you others, then shares the money so they won't dock his pension. But I'm not so stupid as to cover it up, oh no, because nobody gives me the recognition I deserve."

In disgust, Houska hinted that he would show how he recognised his stupidity on payday.

"What makes you do it all?" he asked Cockabogey that evening at home. Cockabogey registered amazement that anyone could be so ignorant and explained that it was its duty to serve whoever hatched it, which it, as a cockabogey, thought perfectly obvious. Its main concern was to see to it that its owner grew rich. If its owner were a craftsman, it would work for him. If a shopkeeper, it would move goods around and put the money in the till. If an officer, Cockabogey would do the shouting for him, while if he worked in an office it would prop his head up during the day to stop him banging it on his desk.

Houska wanted to know if Cockabogey couldn't just bring him money, but the latter rejected the idea, explaining that Houska would get locked up and then Cockabogey would have to rattle his chain for him. Houska's next question – what Cockabogey's contribution would be if his owner was a whore – went unanswered. Houska took that amiss, believing that Cockabogey thought itself superior, so he didn't speak to it all evening. They dined in bilateral silence, after which Cockabogey went to roost in the bed.

The next day, the gang that was working a little way off sent their foreman over to check whether Houska wasn't ill, since he'd stopped going to the pub with them after work. The foreman, Kalivoda, saw on closer inspection that a black fowl was laying the paving stones while Houska kept it supplied with material and fetched the water. That struck him as odd, so he summoned the others. For a while they watched the bird hard at work, but once they registered the rate at which it was working, they banded together and started railing at Houska for using it to upset their quotas; that way no one would earn anything. They also accused him of lacking solidarity and being greedy.

Houska defended himself. He pointed to Cockabogey, who hadn't joined in the discussion because it was still busy at work, and when it ran out of materials, busied itself with sorting the mosaic blocks into black and red. Cockabogey inspired general disgust and Kalivoda threw a stone at it. It dodged and with a single sweep of its half-feathered wings flew up onto Kalivoda's head and shat on him.

Because of the dreadful smell they wouldn't let Kalivoda onto the tram home and he had to walk all the way. Next day, for the same reason, he arrived late for work because he lived miles away, in Kobylisy. Not knowing what to do, he called in sick and roamed the waste dumps of the outer suburbs, because his wife didn't want him indoors and he couldn't enter a pub.

The others were intimated by what had befallen him, which put an end to all attempts to insult

Cockabogey. The men took themselves off to the taproom to confer. Meanwhile Cockabogey kept on working, raising Houska's daily earnings to three hundred and sixty-seven crowns and eighty hellers. It said nothing to by-passers who trampled over where he was working, but urged Houska to say something instead. If it thought Houska was not being severe enough, it tore strips off him.

Meanwhile, the men sent a deputation from the taproom to the company HQ to file a complaint against Houska with the head of the paving section. The latter, having been told about the industrious fowl, thought someone was trying to take the mickey, so he kicked the deputation out.

After some time spent wandering up and down or kicking their heels in the corridors the deputation found the payroll officer and demanded that he investigate Houska's earnings. When the final figure was ascertained the payroll officer's eyes nearly popped out of his head. So he set off with his deputies, the people who set quotas and those in charge of time and motion to see Houska's work-site for themselves. They found Houska and his pal

Cockabogey hard at it, the latter having resolved that that day they would clear four hundred crowns.

The payroll officer, overcoming the initial shock, warned Houska that he risked being put on a lower rate since he was only helping out by fetching and carrying, while the real, specialised paving work was being done by the bird, which, incidentally, wasn't even fully qualified. Having been briefed by Cockabogey, who had foreseen trouble of this kind ever since the conflict with Kalivoda, Houska replied that in that case the wages for the job should be paid to Cockabogey, who was in his charge. For good measure, he added that the payroll officer knew bugger-all about the quality of Cockabogey's work.

The payroll officer went back to headquarters with his deputies and requested personnel to add Cockabogey to the payroll, which would mean he could issue a job-sheet for it. However, personnel refused to register Cockabogey for national insurance until it provided them with evidence that it had left its previous job. This raised another question: whether Cockabogey, as Houska's property, wasn't actually a private-sector employee. The payroll officer, pursued by the spectre of Houska's ever rising earnings, sought out the chief engineer.

The chief engineer was sitting in his office smoking a pipe, dressed in a leather anorak and check shirt. He'd seen engineers dressed like that in films and thought it was the right thing to wear; by calling he was a confectioner. He listened to the problem, adopted a severe frown and promised to think about it. Then he summoned the supervisor responsible for Houska and spoke to him thus:

"We have a little problem to solve. How is it with Houska's performance?"

"Oh, he's a good worker, no question."

"All right, but he can't go on making that kind of money."

"But he does get a lot done," said the supervisor, feeling awkward.

"Look here, cut the crap! I know everything anyway."

"That being so, I'll speak plainly because I know you're kind and understanding. The thing is, old Pozner asked me about it – he's got such a small pension – and the lads put it on their own sheet. We're only human, aren't we?"

"That's of no concern to me," said the chief engineer brusquely. "What's the story about that chicken?"

"Chicken, what chicken? Nobody's given me a chicken. I don't accept anything from anybody, it's not allowed. The odd pint maybe, I wouldn't want to offend the lads, but a chicken, no way, I'd be bound to remember."

The chief engineer didn't know what to do, so he dismissed the supervisor with some vague threats and asked for an extraordinary meeting to be convened, at which he raised the matter. While everyone registered surprise, no one overdid it: anyone who shows too much surprise merely betrays a lack of experience.

Inevitably, the management decided that the sheer enthusiasm of the strange chicken should be exploited in the company's interest, but that did raise the question of whether a chicken could be put on the payroll when it hadn't been planned for and the year's budget was exhausted. The payroll

officer also pointed out that with respect to the rate at which the chicken worked, it could not be paid according to standard quotas. Quotas for the work of poultry in the building trade had never been set.

With that, things ceased to be straightforward. Interest in Cockabogey waned and the chief engineer remained alone on the side of progress. He quite liked the idea of Cockabogey because no other company had one, and he roared with some belligerence that he couldn't guarantee that the deadline would be met without it. But because everyone knew it didn't depend on him, no one was intimidated. Unexpectedly, however, his part was taken by the legal adviser.

The legal adviser – as can well be imagined – couldn't give a damn about the chicken; on the other hand he was proud of his own quick-wittedness. Accordingly he moved that Cockabogey be classified as plant, that it be bought as such from Houska and that it be assigned to the engineering division. That idea appealed to everyone and so the motion was passed, with the added clause that special quotas would be calculated to cover Cockabogey as a machine, because the work did not require a particularly high rate of remuneration. The payroll office would be given that responsibility.

Then the manager of the engineering division was roused and informed that he was being assigned one cockabogey. The engineering manager knew nothing about it because he'd been asleep, but for the sake of form objected that it must be some stupid new idea and that it wouldn't work any better than the last one. He was advised of the essence of a cockabogey and his protest that he wasn't running a zoo was unanimously rejected, which brought the meeting to a close.

The purchase of Cockabogey was placed in the hands of the legal adviser, who summoned Houska to him. Houska presented himself at the office without Cockabogey, who had stayed at the site and was beavering away. Houska rejected the notion that Cockabogey was a machine and offered evidence that it was a living creature because it ate and so on.

The legal adviser promptly slapped Houska down.

"You'd do better not saying such things," he advised him, "because you'd be admitting that you're exploiting the work of another. That wouldn't go down well at all."

Houska conceded that it wouldn't go down well. The matter of the purchase price remained unresolved. A dismayed Houska succeeded in getting a conditional deferral to give him time to think it over.

Returning home, he found Cockabogey in a bad mood. It had worked out ex post that the predicted tally of four hundred crowns for the day had fallen short by eight crowns and twenty hellers. He blamed the erratic supply of materials and reproved Houska for gallivanting around in worktime.

Houska explained to it how things stood. Cockabogey brusquely refused to work for the company on the grounds that the company hadn't hatched it, and in reply to Houska's timid enquiry whether it wouldn't mind working at a slower pace, because otherwise everyone would be in trouble, it flew off the handle, squawking, running round in circles and crapping all over the room.

Houska didn't sleep a wink that night. In the morning he took himself off to the health centre, shattered by work and lack of sleep, and was readily given two days off sick. When Cockabogey saw the doctor's note it started grumbling about falling profits and kept on until Houska left the house on the pretext of going to the chemist's.

He came back in about an hour, carrying a huge brindled tomcat under his arm. In the meantime Cockabogey had scrubbed the floor and was covered in cobwebs, having swept the ceiling with its own body. It didn't like the sight of the cat, but was set at ease by the assurance that it was house-trained. After that it ignored the cat, merely scoffing all its food.

The tomcat did not do what Houska had expected of him. It crawled under the bed and in the afternoon, tormented by hunger and fear of Cockabogey, escaped via the window, which the latter had opened to let in some fresh air.

That night Houska slept uneasily, tormented by a fever and troublesome dreams. He only really dropped off as dawn approached, but he wasn't to enjoy it for long: Cockabogey dragged the duvet off him and squawked:

"Get up, bring me the wash-tub and put the water on; I'm going to do the washing!"

"What's the time?" Houska asked in a stupor.

"Six," came the merry reply. "It's morning. The early bird catches the worm," it added didactically and emphasised the point by hopping round the room several times with an off-putting display of energy.

Houska propped himself up on one elbow.

"I've had an idea," he said quietly. "I've worked out how to make more money. Come close so no one can hear us – they'd only be jealous."

Cockabogey hopped up on the edge of the bed, stretched its neck out and tilted its head towards Houska's mouth. Houska flung one arm out from under the duvet and grabbed its long, scrawny neck. He felt it twisting in his hand. Cockabogey fought back with its beak, croaked, writhed and ripped the pillow-case with its talons. Then the movement began to subside, its eyes became veiled with an opaque membrane and its head flopped to one side.

Houska kept hold of the neck a while longer then let go; Cockabogey landed limply on the floor with a thump. Houska turned towards the wall, wriggled about until he got comfortable and drifted into a dreamless sleep.

When he woke up it was late afternoon. He got dressed, wrapped Cockabogey's body in newspaper and headed for the King's Head. There he deposited the bundle on the taproom counter. The barman examined the bird and swept it deftly under the counter.

"Twenty," he said. Houska nodded. He sat down at a corner table, placed a bottle of rum in front of him and started drinking. With only a little left in the bottle he rose and staggered over to the bar.

"Give me a couple of eggs," he said to the barman.

"Hard-boiled?"

"No, raw."

"What d'you want 'em for?"

"I'm goin' to smash 'em," Houska hissed, "to smithereens. I 'ate eggs. I'm going to kick every egg I find to kingdom come," he bellowed fit to fill the saloon. Several of the regulars rose in consternation and made to pay.

"Go home," said the barman.

"I'm not goin' 'ome, I'm not goin' 'ome," Houska whooped. "Not today, not tomorrow, and not the day after either. And I'll be off work without a doctor's note. And they won't pay me any money and it'll be great!"

The barman shook his head in bewilderment.

"They won't pay me at all," Houska sank into daydreaming, "they'll dock everything and even charge me a penalty. And..."

"Stop bragging," a hoarse voice squawked quietly. A head with green eyes and a faded comb peeked out from the shelf behind the barman's back. "No bragging, do you hear? Your sick note expires tomorrow so make sure you're at work on time. And don't forget to pick up your sickness benefit form, or you'll be out of pocket."

Houska lurched out into the fresh air without a word. He staggered helplessly towards a lamp-post, from the lamp-post to the street-corner. At the corner there was a statue. He headed over to it and sank to his knees with a thud next to its base.

"Dear Saint Thaddeus, shield me from the fiends of hell," he mumbled imploringly and immediately added something else, of which the less said the better, because he had registered that the statue wasn't St Thaddeus but Dr Podlipný, the Lord Mayor.

He felt that the entire world was conspiring against him and that he had drunk a great deal of rum.

"I'm the unluckiest man in the world," he pitied himself in an undertone, "so bloody unlucky. And why? What for? I've never hurt a fly, or chicken!"

A dark mass landed on his jacket shoulder. Cockabogey took a moment to get a grip on the fabric and regain its balance.

"Don't lie," it squawked, "that's not true! Who was it tried to strangle me, eh?"

Houska's head sank and he burst into snuffling tears.

"Why are you doing this to me?" he sobbed, "What have I done to you?"

"You tried to wring my neck," Cockabogey reproved him ill-temperedly and twisted its neck. "That's most ill-mannered, and pretty stupid as well. You don't imagine you can kill me, do you?"

"But... what... what am I supposed to do with you?"

"What do you mean, do with me? I do everything myself, don't I?"

"That's just it," Houska sniffed, "you do everything and I'm left to suffer. What sort of a life is that?"

"I can't do your suffering for you," Cockabogey said with some irritation, "I don't know how. God alone knows what else you'd have me do for you!"

Houska shook his head.

"You're a bad bird," he chided it childishly.

"No, I'm not. I can't be. And I can't be good either. I'm Cockabogey, not a reforming protestant. I am what I am and I do what it behoves a cockabogey to do. Only you can be bad or good. All I do is work for you."

"And what am I supposed to do?"

"Whatever you like. I don't care."

Houska stood up with Cockabogey on his shoulder and waved a fist at the clouds in the sky.

"Christ almighty, perishin' fowl, won't I ever be rid of you?"

"You want to be rid of me?" Cockabogey half-opened its amber eyes in surprise.

"For God's sake, why do you think I tried to wring your neck?"

"How should I know. You people are sometimes a bit weird. So you really do want to be rid of me?"

"I really do. Honest. I want to be rid of you, I do. – Does that surprise you?"

"No. I don't care, it's up to you. It's just that if you do want to, just say 'Ugh, ugh, I don't want you'. But you can't take it back afterwards. – Well?"

Houska stood upright. Cockabogey hopped down from his shoulder and stretched its neck out expectantly.

"Ugh, ugh," said Houska "Listen, I didn't mean you any harm."

"I know. You were just being stupid. So then, are you going for it?"

"Ugh, ugh, I don't want you," said Houska resolutely and waited for the earth to open and swallow Cockabogey up. Instead, the hen just turned round calmly and set off along the kerbside. In his surprise Houska took a step after it.

153 THE COCKABOGEY

"I say, what will become of you?" he enquired. Cockabogey looked back and fixed him with a strangely alien stare.

"Cluck-cluck-cluck – ," it went.

"Don't be silly!"

"Cluck-cluckety-cluck-cluck – "

Houska gestured in disgust. It was starting to drizzle. He turned up his collar and strode off towards home.

"– clack-clack," Cockabogey finished off. It squatted down by the base of the statue, half squatted, and with no obvious effort laid an egg.

"Cluck-cluck-cluck-clack," it declared. Then it stood up, shook itself and hopped up onto the statue's head. From there it swung across to a tram wire, suspended itself head down and rode off into the dark flapping its wings.

The egg was lying by a wall, white with black speckling, a bit larger than a hen's.

It began to rain.

It had turned cold towards morning and dew had fallen. He crept out from under the open casement, gripped at the gaps between the pantiles with the gristly spurs of his pointy heels and with a blissful sigh exposed his spindly, almost spider-like limbs to the rays of moonlight. Coming out into the moonlight from time to time was the only thing that gave him any real pleasure. The insects that dropped inside through open dormers and the dew he would lap from the moss-covered tiles before daybreak were nothing special to look forward to. He didn't need much. Anatomically he was so adapted to his particular lifestyle that he never needed to exert himself. His long, spindly legs, disproportionate to the length of his body, were quite up to carrying him from one roof-ridge to the next and along the walkways that ran beside the chimney stacks, the prehensile claws on his legs kept him from slipping, and his long outspread arms were a perfect substitute for a tight-rope walker's pole.

His transparent eyeballs projected more than half-way out of their sockets. His head was fairly

small; he didn't need it much anyway. He didn't think much about what he was doing, acting almost mechanically and being mostly satisfied with just being. During the day he would sleep wedged in the wide gaps between the tiles and roof timbers, where he knew he was free from all disturbance, while at night he would hop across a few roofs for the sheer joy of movement, then find a level spot somewhere to bask in the light of the moon. He had long lost the thrill of hanging from gutters, letting himself down towards attic windows, and hooting *oohoo* and shining his eyeballs to frighten a family at its table or a poor servant girl who, with one stocking in her hand, was dreaming about hussars. The world kept changing, but he remained the same, because he had very little imagination. He was simple. He was of the old school.

He never puzzled over why people sometimes crept out of dormer windows the same way he did, hidden by the dark of night and weighed down with bundles. He used to believe they were having fun, just as his fun were his nocturnal rooftop peregrinations, and before he came finally to terms with the facts – and that was long ago – he would often wonder why they had chosen this kind of pastime when their eyes weren't much good in the dark. He had once boomed *oohoo* at one such man with a bundle, years before, and the idiot had jumped with fright and hurtled to the ground. Doodledor then had his work cut out, hooting his *oohoo* for a long time before he frightened away all those people who had come up to the loft with lamps, led by a fat man with a sash and a feather in his hat, and had poked around the spaces between the beams with nasty, rusty halberds. But that was long ago. Since then he hadn't done it again. He wanted peace and quiet, and he got it.

The dormer right next to him squeaked on its hinges and the frame slowly rose. Another one. Obviously. First he poked his head out, looked about him with stupid, unseeing, human eyes, hauled his bundle out after him, and with ludicrous clumsiness scrabbled along past the chimneys to the way across to the next house, then clambered down over the balcony to the passage between the houses. How ridiculous. One *oohoo* and he would have been down.

Doodledor didn't move. With all the dust and cobwebs he was a shade of grey that almost merged him into one with the blackened tiles even in those nice, bright, warm moonbeams. He was cosy where he lay. If he went to change position the crackle of his bony body would echo out over the uneven roof. He had barely begun to relish the warm delight of the moonlit night when another head appeared framed in the dormer. They're obviously feeling quite energetic tonight. Doodledor expected this one to haul out another bundle. But he didn't. He climbed out alone, but, with no bundle, slightly less awkwardly that the first one; he squirted a nasty yellow light ahead of him and set off along the walkway past the chimneys. His buttons glinted in the moonlight, as did his polished boots and something on his shoulder. He proceeded with caution.

He was right above Doodledor, who was watching the progress of his shiny boots. He would pass on by and peace would descend. Many others had passed before. Then a bit of the rotten gangplank crumbled off right at the edge. One boot was left hanging in mid-air.

"Oohoo," Doodledor hooted and, clamping his claws to the tiles, pulled himself up to his full height. "Oohoo," he trumpeted for all he was worth. "Oohoo, oohoo, oohoo!"

He was terribly afraid the man might slip and tread on his head.

Fortunately the man kept his balance. He wobbled several times, then leaned against the iron rail of the walkway, pulled out some shiny object and made a clicking noise with it.

"Halt! Who goes there?" he said. "Hands up, or I shoot!"

Doodledor shrunk into a little ball. He slipped under the walkway to the other side, but there too the nasty yellow light was seeking him out, and the man repeated his challenge. Doodledor slowly raised his arms towards the moon.

He knew what shooting was and didn't like it. He was afraid of it. It wasn't that long ago that people had been chasing each other over his rooftops, climbing up and falling down, and bits of tiles had kept flying past him and strange things had whizzed and banged and kept him awake. Something had flown straight through the roof right above him, making a hole in one of the beams big enough to stick your thumb in. Then it had stopped. But it was unpleasant and, rather than let it happen again, he was willing to oblige even such a senseless demand as the one the man on the gangway was insisting on.

"Oohoo," he hooted one last time, on the off-chance that it might work. It didn't. Then he stepped out into the light.

The police sergeant yelped and almost dropped his pistol and torch. The thing was so unexpected and so evil-looking, like a huge spider with four legs or an outsize grey skeleton. Its eyeballs were like opaque light-bulbs and from each side of a small round pod a handful of long, dusty hairs hung down almost to its shoulders, except it didn't have proper shoulders. Its raised arms seemed to grow straight out of its neck. It didn't have a recognisable chest. The whole thing looked ghastly, hideous.

The sergeant was embarrassingly aware that he didn't have to climb out onto the roof, and certainly not alone. But there had been far too much cat-burgling of late and it was no joke having to keep listening to the boss saying: "Yes, sergeant, it may seem strange, but cat-burglary is generally carried out by burglars acting like cats. You might find that hard to imagine, but take it from me, it's true!" An old stager with just a year to go before retirement couldn't care less, because they could all go and... But a younger man usually hopes to climb the ladder. And the sergeant did want to climb that ladder. He'd got used to the idea of climbing the ladder. His Amy had also got used to it and kept nagging at him to try harder and climb higher, now he'd made it this far. It was sad for a young man to see his career prospects go up in smoke because there was a cat-burglar going the rounds, and doing it rather well. He and Amy were bound to have more children and he didn't want his children to have a dad who was permanently stuck on the bottom rung. Having a dad who had risen up the ladder is always a good thing. And people should look after their children. It's their duty.

But there was no point standing about on a roof, pointing a gun at a monstrosity that wasn't even offering resistance. He lowered his weapon and returned it to its holster.

"You can put your hands down," he said.

Doodledor let his arms drop down parallel to his sliver of a trunk. He could make his escape now. If he ran up onto the ridge of the roof and down the other side he could get away by following the guttering any way he wished. But he was enjoying himself. No one had ever addressed him directly before. In fact no one had ever spoken to him at all. Sometimes he had regretted the fact. He had often listened to people talking, he understood the sense of the words and had even had a go himself. And he could do it, but talking to himself wasn't the real thing.

The sergeant cleared his throat. He was uneasy. He reached inside his shirt, fished out a packet of cigarettes and extended his hand out towards the creature. Doodledor didn't move. Neither accepting nor rejecting. He didn't know what this was. The sergeant drew back his hand, took out a cigarette and struck a match. Doodledor shrunk away. Could this man mean him harm after all? He didn't like fire. He didn't trust fire.

The sergeant cleared his throat again and drew on his cigarette.

"Forgive me," he said, "I must have confused you with someone else in the dark. Silly of me. I'm up here looking for a thief. There's someone hereabouts who's systematically nicking washing and stuff from people's lofts. I don't get it. What good are a few bits of bed-linen to anybody, especially when you think of the risk? Don't you agree? Anyway, each to his own. By the way, you didn't notice anyone crawling out the window just now, did you?"

"Yes," said Doodledor. The man on the walkway impressed him, because he showed no fear and was speaking to him politely.

He wanted to add that the man who had crawled out of the window a moment before was carrying a bundle, but then had second thoughts. Such a clever man who is not afraid of spooks must surely know that everybody out and about at night on the rooftops carries a bundle.

"What did he look like? Could you describe him?"

"He looked human," said Doodledor. "I think it was a human. It seems highly likely."

"How do you mean?"

"He was carrying a bundle."

"Aha. Which way did he go?"

"Out of here, then along the walkway and down the other side over the balcony."

The sergeant paused for thought. He was no dullard. Obviously, he was intrigued what this spooky thing was doing here and what it actually was. But he was just bright enough not to ask about things a knowledge of which might be of no use to him. He wasn't here to catch spooks, but cat-burglars. His boss wasn't interested in chasing spooks.

"Do you live here permanently?"

"All the time," said Doodledor, thinking that the man was not so bright after all, since he was asking the obvious.

The sergeant sat down on the walkway.

"Come and sit here with me so I don't have to shout."

He quickly lit another cigarette. He suspected that anything as scruffy as this was bound to stink.

Doodledor skipped across the distance to the walkway and, landing with one foot on the edge of it, pulled himself up and sat down next to the man with the shiny buttons. The sergeant registered that the spectre was indeed unbelievably ugly, but, amazingly, did not smell.

"The thing is," he said, "I want to ask you a favour. I'm in a bit of a fix. You say you live here all the time, but I can't, because I've also got things to do down below. Apart from that I've got a family. I've got a little eight-month-old boy. Look," he said, taking out a photograph.

Doodledor knew all about the fuss humans make over their young. They let themselves be tyrannised by them, bill and coo over them, which they also do over one another, but only extremely rarely, and are generally at their beck and call. Doodledor couldn't fathom this, never having been a juvenile. He didn't know what to say or do, because he was afraid the man might not want to talk to him any more.

The sergeant put the photograph away in his wallet. He assumed he had shown sufficient humanity to his interlocutor and so could get down to the matter at hand.

"You see, I simply need your help. I need to find out who this cat-burglar is, and you, well... Of course this will remain our secret, I know you're afraid of encountering prejudice, but at the same time it's your duty to assist us."

He had wanted to say 'civic duty' as he usually did, but then dropped the 'civic'. It probably didn't apply to this spooky creature.

Doodledor was flattered. This was the first human ever to have spoken to him.

"How can I help you?" he asked. That seemed the polite thing. The artist who used to live right under the roof and had died years before had used the words in welcoming the bailiff.

"All I need to know," the sergeant explained, "is the burglar's name. We can take care of the rest."

"So why don't you ask him?" Doodledor wondered. He was naive. He meant no ill.

"Oh dear me. I'm hardly likely to meet him. Your chances of running into him are far better."

Doodledor understood that if he could ascertain the name of the man with the bundle he would be doing the man with the gold buttons a favour. He did *not* understand what the two men had against each other. His greatest concern was for his own peace and quiet. People with bundles seemed to enjoy the protection of other people because on that other occasion, when the man had taken fright and gone tumbling down, others came up onto the roof, most likely to avenge him. Really the very last thing Doodledor wanted was for the loft to be running live with people brandishing torches and halberds.

"What has the man with the bundle done to you?" he asked cautiously.

"Nothing to me personally," the sergeant smiled at his naivety. "But he's a thief. He steals things. Takes things that don't belong to him."

Doodledor had never owned anything. Hence

his view that if someone owned something that mattered to him, he should keep an eye on it. He tried to say as much with all the courtesy he could muster. A shiver went down the sergeant's back. His companion was apparently not only hideous, but totally amoral. But that couldn't be helped. He needed him.

"It's like this," he explained, "if someone's got something he's worked for, nobody else is allowed to take it from him. When someone wants something, whatever it might be, he must work honestly to earn it, which means he mustn't take it from someone else or force anyone else to slog away on his behalf."

Doodledor hung on his every word. He was having fun. He thought the world a deal more interesting once you understood how it was run.

"And what else isn't allowed?"

The sergeant felt slightly awkward again. He couldn't recite the whole criminal law to a spook. For one thing, there wasn't the time, and for another, he wasn't in the mood.

"Oh there's lots," he tried. "But mostly it'll never

have any bearing on you. Stealing's not allowed, whether from lofts or anywhere else, or killing, or saying things that aren't true, and it's not allowed to cheat people of things they've been promised or exploit their labour for private gain."

"And do all people know that?"

"They all know it, but they don't always observe it. The ones that don't are wicked and everybody else has to help prevent such wickedness succeeding."

The sergeant had never been called on to explain these things before, so he was explaining them as you might to a child.

Doodledor finally understood that all those people he'd seen over the years creeping past him with their bundles were wicked, and he regretted not knowing that before. He mused that the one who fell had taken fright because he was wicked, while this man wasn't afraid of him because he wasn't wicked and probably wasn't worried about things done by good people.

The outcome of these musings was the greatest offer he had ever made in his life:

"Next time he comes by, I'll go *oohoo*," he said, roaring out his 'oohoo' so vehemently that the sergeant almost fell off the walkway. "He'll get the shock of his life, fall down and be no more trouble to anyone. Shall I?"

"That won't be necessary," said the sergeant. "His name will be enough. It'll be better that way."

Apart from being totally lacking in bloodlust, he was led to this attitude by a practical consideration: a gamekeeper gets his reward if he brings in no more than a cat's snout, and no one asks how the cat died. But his boss wants the cat-burglar alive. He would definitely not be chuffed at the snout of a burglar killed by falling off a roof.

"And will you be glad?"

"It's not me that matters. It's in the interest of society. But of course I'll be glad as well. So we're agreed. I'll come up here every night about this time, I'll wait for you on this walkway, and you'll tell me what you've found out."

He overcame his revulsion and offered the monster his hand, clad in a leather glove. Doodledor didn't understand, but he wasn't afraid, because the man who had been telling him about the world of people was his friend. He let his claw-ended limb be squeezed by the leather of the glove. The sergeant rose and rubbed his chilled knees with his hands. It was morning. The first light of dawn glimmered between the chimneys.

The next two nights nothing happened. The sergeant came in vain and left in disappointment. Doodledor was very upset, but also glad that his friend had stopped by for a chat. He had begun to relish conversations about what was good and what wasn't. If spooks could blossom, he would have burst into bloom like a rose-bush over those two nights. For the first time, he felt that existence wasn't entirely pointless, because he had learned that any act can be classified somehow, and in addition he had a job to perform.

On the third night the job was done. It was embarrassingly simple.

Shortly after his friend left, he heard some hinges squeaking from about four roofs away. He scampered off after the sound. It had been raining and the roofs were damp. He banged one knee slightly, never having had to run that fast after rain, but he managed to reach the spot just as the man was closing the dormer window behind him and bending to pick up the bundle he had set down beside him. Doodledor didn't intend to frighten him: his friend didn't want the man with the bundle to fall off the roof. So he squatted behind a chimney and, recalling what the done thing is in such circumstances, bellowed:

"Hands up, or I shoot!"

The man with the bundle glanced into the darkness, but he couldn't make out the figure from which the voice had come. It was a good way off across the wet roof.

"Come off it, guv!" he said jovially. He was no novice, so he knew that hardly anyone in the land carried a weapon, and if anyone did then he wasn't going to use it to send a chap streetwards for the sake of a few bits of bed-linen and a dismantled sewing machine.

"Hands up," Doodledor repeated the magic formula, of whose potency he was unshakeably convinced.

"Shit!" said the man with the bundle. Downwards from the chimney whence the voice came the roof sloped steeply and offered nothing to get a purchase on. His pursuer would have to slide straight down on his arse, and if he didn't manage to grab hold of the gutter, which the man with the bundle would not recommend, he would end up in the yard among the dustbins. Then they could come and scrape him up in the morning.

He grabbed his bundle and slung it over his shoulder. He sensed he had the upper hand, because he knew the lie of the land. If there was someone waiting down below – and there wasn't, otherwise Tony would have whistled – then that bloke behind the chimney presented no greater threat than a gingerbread devil. He stepped out onto the walkway.

Doodledor was desperate. If the man with the bundle escaped, his friend would be angry and never come and talk to him again. The man with the bundle might never come back – he must have given him a shock – and Doodledor would lose a friend because he hadn't done what he had promised. He could reach the man with a few bounds. But what if he so frightened him that he fell to the ground? His friend didn't want that.

Meanwhile, the man with the bundle had reached the end of the walkway. He was so sure of himself that he didn't even look back. Then he hung the bundle round his neck and was descending the iron ladder towards the little platform that bridged the gap between the two gables of the old building. Doodledor spread out his arms and broke into a run along the ridge of the roof. All he could do now was jump down onto the platform – but in such a way as to land between the man and the edge of the platform so that he could grab him if he startled him and the man seemed about to fall.

The platform was quite small. It was damp from the rain and the old cement was crumbling at its edges. Doodledor didn't know whether he could get killed. He had never given it any thought. But experience had taught him that he was capable of doing himself an injury like anyone else if he wasn't careful and if his gift of equilibrium and skill at grabbing onto things with his talons didn't save him. Until that day he had never done anything the least bit risky. He'd never had to. Now he did. He crouched and jumped.

The man with the bundle spotted something flying through the air from the ridge. Then it landed right in front of him, looking like a huge twisted spider. Finally it stood erect in the moonlight.

"Oohoo," Doodledor bellowed. He had been storing a lungful of breath all the way down.

The man dropped his bundle and pressed his back up against the damp plaster of the gable. He could feel the rendering crumbling under his fingers as he dug into it, convulsed with terror. Then he bellowed in turn. Never in his life had he seen anything so fearsome as the figure that now reared up in front of him on the edge of the platform, silhouetted against the night sky.

"Oohoo," Doodledor repeated, rather pleased that his traditional weapon had won the day. The man in front of him had stopped bellowing and was now just wheezing in utter terror. Then he raised his arms. He was surrendering. Doodledor looked him over with some satisfaction. So wicked people were afraid.

"What's your name?" he asked and had to repeat it twice more because the wicked man was so afraid that he couldn't answer.

"Bohumil Kepka," he stuttered finally.

That was that. Job done. Doodledor picked up the bundle, ran up the roof with it and stowed it behind a chimney. He had his work cut out because he was slight of frame and not used to carrying anything heavy. Then he slipped into the nearest loft, crawled behind a beam and, with some time to go before dawn, fell asleep immediately. He couldn't have cared less that Bohumil Kepka's hands were shaking and his knees knocking so violently that it took him over three-quarters of an hour to scramble down to the yard.

"Bohumil Kepka," Doodledor reported the following night. He was all a-quiver with suppressed pride. The sergeant grew grave.

"Who'd have thought it! Are you sure you're right? He lives right here in the next block, and he's a roofer... hm, we'll give him the once over!"

And when the sergeant came back onto the roof the following night, Doodledor, sensitive to light as he was, thought that his friend's eyes were shining even more than his boots, buttons and everything else.

"Not only has he confessed," the sergeant reported, "but we found bits and pieces left over from previous weeks. But he swears blind," he was almost choking with emotion, "that he'd been going to give it up anyway. He said he'd seen a ghost on the roof yesterday and wild horses wouldn't get him back on the roof now. Listen, my friend," he added, slipping into a tone of intimacy Doodledor hadn't yet heard from him, "without you we could have waited an eternity before catching him. He knows his stuff. But it was really good of you to help us."

With people, he would usually clap a hand on their shoulder at moments like this. This time there was no shoulder available, so he merely placed one hand on the monster's bony neck, gave it a gentle, friendly squeeze and a shake.

"It was my duty," said Doodledor. He was

pleased at being praised and at having been of assistance, now that he understood the ways of the world in which it had befallen him to dwell.

"Yes, yes," said the sergeant, "I know. And also the labourer is worthy of his hire, as the saying goes. That might not be quite so easy to deal with in your case, but think a bit, is there something that you'd like? Provided it's within my power of course. But even if not, I'd put a word in... The thing is, I might need your help for a while longer. There are a few more cat burglars active in Prague and after this success I've been put in charge... But I'll let you know when the time's ripe. For now though, tell me what you'd like from me."

Doodledor felt his skin stretching and crinkling under its layer of dust and cobwebs. He was being granted a wish. He'd never wished for anything before. For the first time he had that feeling we get when there's a chance of something we haven't dared wish for for a very long time. It is a strange sensation because the chance of having a wish fulfilled is sweetest before time and contemplation take the gloss of novelty off it.

"Well?" said the sergeant. Doodledor turned his eyes full of devotion and uncertainty towards him.

"If I might..." Then he came out with it: "I'd like to spend some time with humans. Even just once. To see how they live, how they talk among themselves, but not from up here on the roof, to talk with them, because... it must be ever so nice."

The sergeant laughed happily, like a boy. He was glad there was no more to it than that.

"That I can promise you. Yes, definitely. You've deserved it. Since it means so much to you, of course I'll keep coming to see you, even if we won't actually be working together. For as long as you wish. And once we're done with the business we have to deal with next, I'll take you home with me one night and we can chat all night long. And you can tell my little boy all about roofs, all the things you've seen up here, and this and that. Are you pleased? Yes? See, anything goes. So goodbye for now."

He shook Doodledor by the neck one last time and disappeared through the window into the loft space.

Night was getting into full swing. The moon cast down its munificent rays, but Doodledor knew that that night he wouldn't be able to bask idly in them. He was brimful of happiness. Too much had been going on for him to cope with solitude. He climbed down to the gutter, leaned out over the street and watched as his friend came out of the street door and lit a cigarette. Moving from gutter to gutter he followed his progress from above, sometimes gripping hold of a tile, and finally ran across a telephone wire to the other side of the street, dancing with outstretched arms each time he changed his footing. He ran across the rooftops of several blocks and finally his eyes followed a drain-pipe down towards the street door that his friend was just unlocking.

About two floors down below the gutter the lights were on in three windows in the façade of the building. Doodledor hung down from the gutter, then, pressing his back against the drain-pipe and clamping his claws round the sheath that protected the lightning conductor, he slithered down until he was level with the lighted windows. Then he hopped onto a window-ledge. The window was half-open. Concealed by the edge of the wall, he settled down on the ledge and rested his arms between his legs.

A young woman in an apron, her fair hair trimmed neatly about her chubby cheeks, was sitting at a table sewing. Then the door opened and his friend walked in. He was wearing a grey knitted cardigan and on his feet he had, instead of shiny boots, some flat-soled slippers. The woman looked up.

"Have you taken your boots off? That's good. Listen, I've bought you some veal for Sunday."

Doodledor's friend gave her a kiss, sat down at the table and lit a cigarette.

"The boss gave me a commendation for that Kepka chap," he said contentedly. He pulled the ashtray towards him and leaned back comfortably on his chair.

"And quite right too," said the woman. "He should count his blessings that he's got you. It's taken him long enough to realise." She stuck her needle in and did another stitch. "The baby hasn't been eating properly today."

"What?" Doodledor's friend got up from the table, went over to the white-decked cot and pulled back the coverlet under which his juvenile was sleeping. Doodledor had no affinity with human juveniles, but this one was an exception. One day he would be telling it all about the things he had seen on the rooftops. He would rehearse long and hard so as to make a good go of it. This juvenile was bound to be as good as its father and his, Doodledor's, friend.

"He looks all right," his friend appraised his juvenile.

"Why shouldn't he?" asked the woman. "He just hasn't eaten much. Less than normal. He usually eats more than other babies."

She went over to the cot and picked the baby up in her arms.

"Coo-coo-coo," said Doodledor's friend, tickling its chubby cheeks.

"The boss said," his friend went on, "that I might even be considered for promotion. The Kepka business was a stroke of genius."

"Praise be," said the woman, dandling the juvenile. "Little Georgie and I are really pleased. I hope you didn't tell him how it was. Or did you?"

"Don't be silly! I'm not stupid."

"I knew you'd do the right thing. How *did* you explain it?"

"Patient observation. I'd had my suspicions and followed them up. That's what he likes to hear. What on earth was I supposed to tell him?"

"Of course," the woman agreed. "You can't talk sense to him. He's a stickler for the rule book and doesn't care about people's families. You should try for a transfer. Look at Vaníček – he's already an inspector. See Georgie, it's your daddy! But I tell you, that business with the spook or whatever, I still don't like it much. Don't go blabbing about it anywhere else. What would people think of us? As it is, old Mrs Kučera keeps going on about you being out at all hours of the night and how she pities me, understand? And hinting whether your shifts really are that long. But I told her, look missus, I said – you know she doesn't like being called missus, so I say it on purpose – look missus, I trust my husband because he's a decent, honest man with nothing to hide, not like some people who are all sweetness and light at home and once out of sight start baring their toothy grins like broken combs at every woman that passes. That was a good one, wasn't it? You know her old man has a front tooth missing, don't you? You've seen him. But this gadding about at night has to stop soon. Little Georgie won't be able to enjoy his father, and if anyone gets to hear... I mean about your spook. As long as you need it, keep it going for all I care, but then get rid of it. It won't do you any good. You've got a decent job and some people might envy us."

Doodledor's good friend smiled at his wife and stroked her hair.

"Of course, dear. It's a good thing I can tell you everything; you're not like other women who start imagining all sorts of nonsense. I know where my duty lies – to you and little Georgie. I'm not going to risk becoming a laughing stock down at the station. But I tell you, it's been damn' difficult sometimes, that ghoul is *so* hideous!"

"Ugh!" his wife shuddered and snuggled up

close to him. "Don't talk about it. It always makes me glad I'm not a man when I hear things like that."

"Don't you worry about it. I'll get rid of it somehow when it's over. It can't leave the roof, and it seems awfully old anyway. And sort of manky. And it's so stupid it believes everything you tell it. It won't give me any trouble, you can be sure of that. Otherwise I wouldn't have started it. But forget it for now, let's not spoil the evening since it's such an ugly brute – and you're so pretty! Come on now, who's my little sweetie?"

Doodledor levered down on his bent knees and slowly stood up. He wasn't agitated. In his mind he went over the human code as it had been instilled in him, word by word, and felt that he could never give it up. You can only live without it until you've had first-hand experience of it. He knew now what was wicked and what was good. He'd been told. But he didn't quite know what to make of it. To promise something then not do it, to exploit the work of another for one's own gain – that was all wicked. They'd told him it was wicked. And they'd

also told him something else: that everyone must fight so that such wickedness couldn't succeed, otherwise the world would become infested with those things that he knew in his mind to be wicked.

He knew that he must take steps. But what steps, he didn't know. He would dearly have liked to stick his head through the window and go 'Oohoo!', pulling the most terrible faces he could muster, so that that plump juvenile would wake up, remember it to its dying day and be driven to ask about it one day. But he resisted the temptation. Suppose they shot at him? But no, they wouldn't, because they thought they still needed him, and then there would be the risk that everyone would discover what human nests are made of. But that still wouldn't do the trick.

Slowly he hauled himself back up the drain-pipe onto the roof. Unhurriedly. He opened a dormer and slipped down into the loft space. He took a huge piece of white cloth down from a line, spread it out on the floor, piled onto it all the other pieces of cloth he could find, made a bundle of them, then crawled back out of the window and, bent double under the weight, set off across the roof. He didn't know where to take it, but he did know he was going to take it away somewhere where no one would find it. And the same thing tomorrow, and the day after. He viewed it as a duty, because he had understood everything. For he lacked imagination. He was only a spook. And he did have such a small head.

COOKIE

"Anything else there?" the editor, a Mr Kotlach, asked. The question was pretty much a mechanical one; he wasn't really hoping there would be. All around it was the same: damp, mildew in places, and dripping with water.

The man in black oilskins squirmed as a drip from the ceiling went down his neck.

"Nothing else," he said grumpily, "only some old cellars. We'll have it bricked up, and there's nothing to see anyway."

The man in oilskins was a rat-catcher. He was paid to destroy rats, so that's what he did. He had no special liking for the journalists who came down into the sewers from time to time and then wrote about it. The point was that in order to boost his standard of living he would sell the rats he caught in the sewers to research institutes, and the journalists would frighten them away. Apart from that, it's not without relevance that rat-catching is paid at piece rates, while interviews with gentlemen of the press are only paid by the hour.

"But I can take a look, can't I?" Kotlach persisted. He was game for anything as long as it produced a decent article. Up to now, autumn had been on the bland side. He had always thought it a bit of a fraud that cellars, underground passages and other such places contained no pirate treasures, long-forgotten art collections or at least a walled-up nun. Any normal man has a touch of the romantic to him, and only the most dogged hack could fight world-weariness by churning out arty-farty pieces about the ducks on the river or problems with the bus service.

"S'pose so," the rat-catcher replied. "Take this lamp and mind you don't get your boots full o' crap. They've got to go back clean, and it was me who signed for 'em. But I'm not goin' in there with you. It's not how I get my kicks. And don't go too far in, there's nothin' to see."

The journalist ran the funnel of light from the lamp across the putrefying vaulted roof. He had no grounds for not believing the rat-catcher, but at the same time he knew that the public couldn't be sated with percentages of industrial outputs. Sloshing through the greenish water in his borrowed boots, he passed round several bends. After about fifty metres the passage opened out into a multi-vaulted vastness. There were about five separate spaces and recesses. As was to have been expected, none led anywhere. Except that close to the ground there were several holes, just about big enough for a largish dog to crawl through. Out of a sense of duty the editor shone his light into each of them, did one last sweep of the whole uninspiring place and turned to go back. Now he would have to take the rat-catcher for a pint and talk to him about rats. Not that there would be much point. The rat-catcher would never tell him the truth. Being an expert, he would go on in his discerning, tedious way about how things should be done, not how they were.

Thoroughly fed up, he trundled his way across the mouldering brick floor in his musketeer's top boots, whose laces were attached at the upper end to his belt.

"Ehem, ehem," someone coughed politely from his left. "Excuse me, sir..."

The journalist turned and pointed the light in the direction of the voice. By one crumbling recess – one of those from which a hole led downwards somewhere – stood a dwarf, about two feet tall. He wasn't ugly and he wasn't even frightening. He was wearing a little red suit, a bit scruffy and darker than it had once been, calf-length boots on his feet, and a wide leather belt round his waist. Like a rather tubby gnome, but of serious mien.

"Can I help you?" Kotlach asked courteously. He too was a bit on the plump side and was subconsciously well disposed to all stout people.

The dwarf doffed his tall black hat, adorned with faded gold piping, and gave a touchingly awkward little bow. He was beardless, almost bald, with kindly eyes beneath tortoise-like eyelids. A bit like one of Disney's, Kotlach thought.

The manikin bestowed a friendly smile on him and clasped his hat to his breast.

"Cookie, at your service."

"Kotlach, editor."

"Most pleased to meet you," said the dwarf and bowed once more. "Do forgive me for troubling you, but I merely wished to ask if I could perhaps be of service to you. If I can, I should be only too pleased to oblige. It will be an honour."

"I couldn't say," Mr Kotlach said, unsure of himself. He was by now so spoilt by the permanent shortage of anything out of the ordinary that it was slow to dawn on him that something wasn't quite right here.

"Are you sure there isn't something?" the gnome said sadly. "I'm so very sorry. The thing is, hardly anyone ever comes here, nobody at all of late, and so I just don't get the chance to strut my stuff, as the saying goes. It's so boring! I'd love to do something for you, just a little something. To keep my hand in."

"And what's your line, if you don't mind my asking?" the editor asked. On the one hand, it had occurred to him that he might get something useful out of the dwarf, though it was unlikely that the information would be any good, given that dwarves don't exist, and on the other hand, he was a big softie and couldn't bear to turn someone down. "What is your particular field of expertise?"

He didn't usually resort to such high-flown turns of phrase, but the dwarf seemed to be at home in that style, being of the old school.

"If you please," the dwarf brightened, adding with an ingenuous smile: "I kill people."

"What?" the editor froze.

"Yes, yes, that's right. I kill people," Cookie explained sweetly. "See," he reached behind him into the recess and withdrew from it an iron cudgel with a long, well-worn, wooden handle. "Here's the cudgel I use. I wallop them over the head with it, just behind the ears, and there's your corpse. It's all over in no time, before you can count five."

Mr Kotlach set the light down beside him and opened his pen-knife. He was hoping he would be able to hold the little man off until the rat-catcher could reach him.

He reckoned the rat-catcher would be in no hurry if he knew what was going on.

"Come, come, sir," Cookie pursed his little lips into a comical grimace. "I was in no mind to hurt you! I wouldn't have been telling you otherwise. I only kill to order; I never hurt people on my own account. I couldn't anyway, it's not in my nature. – So, who would you like to be rid of, sir?"

The journalist hesitated, snapped the knife shut and returned it to his pocket. Taking all in all, Cookie did not strike him as aggressive.

"I..., you see," he said uncertainly, "I'm not sure if you could even..."

"But of course," Cookie sought to rally him, "I know I don't look up to it, but that is only the first impression. I have had plenty of practice, so I know where to strike so that death is guaranteed. This cudgel sits beautifully in the hand and it has a nice long shaft. And if necessary I can jump up. Watch!"

Hop! – and he leapt up a good two feet, brandishing the cudgel in the air.

"Well I'll be...," said Kotlach, loosening his cravat. Unless he was fibbing, Cookie was a truly murderous character. Yet he looked so mild and good-naturedly ingenuous that only someone without a shred of decency would dream of harming him.

"Yes, sir," said Cookie with pride, "that's the way to do it! Right behind the ears. And it has been years since I killed anyone! It would drive a fellow to despair. Do say you won't turn me down. I ask nothing in return, it is my sacred obligation. All I need is that modicum of pride in a job well done. And I do do a good job!"

Kotlach wrestled beneath his waterproof to extract his pipe from his pocket, then lit it slowly. It would be unwise to provoke Cookie. He could do a lot of damage with that cudgel of his. But leave him here and wait until some homicidal maniac hired him... A fine mess that would be; your mass murderer, and then Cookie with his sheer enthusiasm! Give them a fortnight and we could be talking rivers of blood.

"Look here," he began tactically, "Mr Cookie..."

"Just Cookie, if you don't mind," the little dwarf said modestly. His demeanour was rather like that of the old menservants you find in stately homes.

"So look here, Cookie," Kotlach improvised. "I don't have anyone for you right now; I hadn't counted on finding you. Apart from that, this isn't the right place."

"Yes, sir, of course, sir," said Cookie.

"Enough. And another thing. Can you give me an assurance that once we do agree you'll be working exclusively for me?"

"Oh but sir," Cookie pronounced reproachfully. "One cannot serve two masters! You can make enquiries about me if you wish. And if you don't have any work for me this minute, please do not let that concern you. I am sure you have much else to worry about. If you are kind enough to avail yourself of my services, I will always remain within earshot. You need not worry about me; I have my means. As soon as the need arises, you will just call 'Cookie', and I'll be there. But to avoid any misunderstanding I will ask: 'Your wish?' I'll skip the 'sir' to keep it brief. And you will say: 'The one at my back, grab your cudgel, kill him!' Please always stand with your back to the person you wish put down, because my eyesight's failing and I would find it hard to find my bearings with a lot of people around. You can leave the rest to me. Do not concern yourself about my discretion; I'm not doing this for the first time. And anyway, who would believe me? There have never been any problems wherever I have lent a hand. Many gentlemen have spoken highly of me, if I may be so immodest."

A shiver ran from the small of Mr Kotlach's back right up to the nape of his neck. Cookie had no equal when it came to talking about murder, which might just as well have been about currant buns.

He could only manage a few indistinct words, but Cookie was content. He took up his cudgel, doffed his hat, shuffled one foot, bowed and disappeared down his hole.

After that, Kotlach barely registered what the rat-catcher was telling him about rats, and the latter had to remind him a couple of times, and with some delicacy, before Kotlach paid for his beer, two shorts and a plate of sausage and onions. That annoyed the rat-catcher, who later complained to the chief vermin exterminator somewhat bitterly about the ingratitude of pressmen.

Kotlach returned to his office. Everyone knew he had been down in the sewers and they made a great show of covering their noses, but he didn't mind. Fat men always get laughed at. If they have any sense, they laugh along with the rest.

"I stink, I stink," he brayed up and down the corridor, then crept into his cubby-hole and sat down to type. Everything that had befallen him that day seemed slightly odd, so he let his imagination run riot. Instead of explaining about bait, poisons and cement mixed with slivers of glass, he started on about what people – as he knew from talking to them – imagined it was like in underground passages. He paid lip-service to realism by describing Cookie, though obviously saying nothing of his unusual pastime, and managed to spin it out to more than five pages. He handed it in and went home.

On the way he whistled happily. It was an autumn afternoon and the sun was shining.

In the hall he bumped into Mrs Hammernick. Mrs Hammernick was the wife of Mr Hammernick and mistress of half of the divided house, the other half of which was inhabited by Mr Kotlach and his two children.

"I say, Mr Kotlach," Mrs Hammernick began, and started rattling on: "ratatatatat..."

"Of course," he said, went into his room and closed the door behind him. It might have been about the phone or the dustbins. Most likely the phone. Mrs Hammernick couldn't pay the whole phone bill because it was so expensive. She couldn't have the phone in the hall, because it would be too far for her to go, and she was unwilling to take other people's calls or let other people into her half of the flat. Mr Kotlach used to insist that none of that made much sense. Mrs Hammernick would say why not. If Mr Hammernick were there, he would show them. But Mr Hammernick wasn't there, being presently detained for his convictions at the President's pleasure. That was distinctly unfair, given that he had suffered similarly during the war, then once more, and again now. Mr Hammernick stole animal pelts from work and sold them on the side.

Mr Kotlach settled into his armchair. First to appear was his son George.

"Daddy!"

"Yes, son?"

"What's new?"

"Not much. What about you?"

"Mrs Hammernick slapped me."

"Oh she did, did she. And why would she do that?"

"I told her she was a whore."

"Then she did right. You shouldn't say such things, especially when they're not true, because Mrs Hammernick is fairly elderly."

"But, Daddy, before that Mrs Hammernick said you're a good-for-nothing who's growing fat at the expense of her work-worn hands. She said it down at the corner. Joe heard her. And she also said she wouldn't be the least bit surprised if Mummy found some other bloke, which she probably had done already, because that's probably the only thing she ever thinks about."

"I see. And where is Mummy?"

"She's out. Mrs Hammernick picked up Joe's teddy-bear in the corridor and threw it down the toilet. She said she didn't want stuff cluttering up the flat."

"So Mummy's gone to buy a new teddy?"

"Noooo. She's gone to get a plumber. It was the little teddy, the grey one, and it must have got stuck right down because the toilet won't flush."

"Aha. And what else has Mrs Hammernick done?"

"She slapped Joe. After Mummy went out he started crying about his teddy. Mrs Hammernick said she wouldn't stand for such noise in the flat."

"Good, son. Go in the other room and get on with your homework. If you need to go to the toilet, use the chamber-pot. Don't go out into the hall, or Mrs Hammernick will throw *you* down the toilet."

Then Mr Kotlach examined his son's swollen lips and settled down with his beloved Anatole France. He was just enjoying the level-headed scepticism of the Governor of Judaea when his wife entered. He put his book down.

"Good evening, darling. Did you find a plumber?"

His wife looked at him like something a badly house-trained dog had brought in, went passed him and opened the door to the next room.

"Georgie, pop down to the Wallace's and ask them to let you have their key for a week, and the key to the loo on their balcony. The plumbers haven't got time. Put your coat and shoes on so you don't catch cold."

"I didn't manage to get a plumber, dear," she explained after George had left. "But I do seem to have managed to marry an ass. What other man would let his wife be insulted like that? Do you know what Mrs Hammernick's been saying again?"

"Yes, my dear. Mrs Hammernick said I am growing fat at the expense of her work-worn hands and that she was surprised you haven't found another bloke."

"That as well. And I think that an idle brain is the devil's workshop. But that was what she said in the morning. This afternoon she went one further and said that I send the boys out after school looking for punters for me, which I could get away with, my husband being on a newspaper. Another woman wouldn't be so lucky. I got this from the plumber, who had it from his wife. The plumber said he didn't believe it much himself, because it didn't seem likely, but he wouldn't be giving evidence in court, nor his wife, because they're too busy and don't fancy the hassle. What do you say to that, Sir Galahad?"

"I think, my dear, that it is illogical. I can't be getting fat at the expense of Mrs H.'s work-worn hands, because her hands are not work-worn. By the same token, I don't believe..."

"And by the same token, you don't believe," his wife's voice rose, "that I could send the boys out looking for punters, because I'd never get even a drunken sailor into a flat where the toilet won't flush. That, as I see it, is your logic. Go and tell the plumber to spread it around, because I... I don't have a life! Eight years, and you still haven't managed to find a different flat. You can't be a real man if you can leave things the way they are!"

She slumped down onto the settee, right on top of his open book, a very picture of disconsolation, a pretty, but deeply unhappy picture.

"Don't you worry about it, Mrs Kotlach," Mrs Hammernick poked her head round the door. "You'll be able to catch up once they clear the bog for you! But I hope it don't take long, I'm not used to slovenliness. – Mr Kotlach, you're wanted on the phone. I told them I'd fetch you, if you're not pissed. But I can't be 'aving' this. I don't mind obligin', but I won't be put upon all the time. I'm entitled to my privacy, whatever government's in power."

Mr Kotlach crossed the hallway and picked up the receiver, which was lying on the crocheted mat of the bedside table between a little water-spaniel and an Andalusian girl with a low-cut neckline.

"Kotlach."

"You took your time! Muntzlinger here. You're not drunk then?"

"No, I'm not," said Mr Kotlach. Muntzlinger was deputy chief editor.

"They didn't seem so sure at your end. And you weren't drunk this afternoon either? You didn't go out boozing with those rodent people, did you? No? So get off your arse and haul it over here. I need to talk to you. You won't regret it."

"Your wife's in the sittin'-room, cryin'," Mrs Hammernick declared. "I reckon this ain't the best time to be goin' off with your drinkin' pals. All I can say is that I'm not in the least surprised your wife enjoys herself where and when she can. I'd say as much to the neighbours, if it came to it. And I'll tell the powers that be. Somebody's going to have to look into this, all the things that go on 'ere, you can be sure of that! You can't keep hidin' behind your job!"

"Listen here..."

"You'll see, you'll see," said Mrs Hammernick and slammed the door. Mr Kotlach opened the door to his sitting-room and seeing the trickle of tears all the way from the settee to the window, closed it carefully again and took his coat off the stand.

Between the cupboards in the hallway he caught a glimpse of faded gold trim on a black hat.

"Excuse me, sir," said Cookie politely, doffing his hat, "are my services not required? A moment ago I heard some noise..."

Mr Kotlach fixed the dwarf with half-seeing eyes.

"No," he sighed, "not at the moment. Thank you, Cookie."

The deputy editor, Muntzlinger, was good at his job. He was held in high regard. And rightly so. Admittedly he didn't do much writing, but he was a dry old fart and that went well for him. People are not judged by what they do well, since that's their job, but by the mistakes they make. Muntzlinger didn't make mistakes, so he wasn't judged. Nor did he commit any acts of heroism. Averagely progressive staff are the backbone of every workplace.

There may be some slight disgrace in wearing spectacles and being a dry old fart at the same time, but Muntzlinger did wear glasses. Nice ones. Not the kind cobblers wear, the kind you get on the national health, nor those fancy foreign ones with wide frames. No, his were nice, neat and averagely progressive. He was just in the process of cleaning them.

He was very kind. First he explained the difference between a feuilleton and a report. Then he explained what fell into neither category. Then he explained the right attitude to take to political spin and, having said all that, he asked:

"Did you go into the sewers?"

"Yes, I did," said Kotlach.

"So we can take that as read. We sent you there so that you could describe what is being done down there to improve working methods. And what did you bring back, having spent a whole day there? What did you write for us, no, not us, for the readers? This is what you wrote!"

"I..."

"Yes, I'm sure. But I haven't finished speaking yet. Don't get me wrong, you know I wish you no ill, but this is what happens when you fritter the day away. I'm not saying you did fritter it away, I don't mean to be unjust, but what you've written reads as if you did fritter it away, which amounts to the same thing. See?"

"I don't really think so," Kotlach protested. "But if you do, I'll take it back and see if I can change a thing or two."

"There's nothing to change. You're going to sit down and re-write it, since you claim you were there. You won't be doing us a favour. And we'll put this thing up on the wall so everyone can read it. With your permission, I'll underline some parts of it. This is not a sanction, just a refinement of ideas. You wrote it for publication, and what I'm suggesting is publishing after a fashion."

"I don't see anything wrong with that," said Kotlach.

"There we have it. It's best to nip things in the bud. Dwarves, gnomes, flight from reality. A good idea for some. Is there anything strange going on at home?"

"I'm nobody's fool," said Kotlach. "And if I am, then within limits."

"My view exactly," said Muntzlinger. "As you say, you're nobody's fool. You're clever enough. But you have to understand that between being clever and being clever-clever there is a difference. Seeing dwarves may be either entirely inadvertent, in which case it's induced by alcohol, or slightly deliberate – if only to avoid seeing something else that your purist intellectual might not think arty-farty enough. It's the duty of each of us to ponder well why we see dwarves!"

Mr Kotlach went out into the corridor, lit his empty pipe and then put it away again.

"Cookie," he said in a low voice, stressing the second syllable.

Cookie shot out of the washroom, dragging his cudgel behind him.

"Your wish?" he asked, all keen, and raised his artless eyes to Kotlach with an expression of anticipation. Mr Kotlach ran his hand across his brow.

"Nothing, nothing," he said hoarsely, "sorry, I didn't mean to call you. Please carry on as if nothing has happened."

"Never mind, sir," said Cookie, ruefully.

Two hours later, Kotlach placed four typewritten sheets on the secretary's desk, locked up and hung the keys on the board. His feuilleton addressed the important place of vermin extermination in urban hygiene, and related progress in this sphere to progress in other spheres. It was a most instructive feuilleton. It bore the title: *Workers Beneath the Surface*.

By the time he came out into the street it was already dark. It wasn't really late, but the light fails earlier in the autumn. Neon lights winked and blinked and there was a smell of rotting leaves in the air. Mr Kotlach stuck his hands in the pockets of his unbuttoned coat and sauntered slowly off to his local stand-up café. He was wondering whether he could find a bit of wire at home. If he bent the end of a wire to form a hook, he could fish the stupid little grey-plush teddy-bear out of the toilet.

"Coffee, please," he said arriving at the counter. As if stung by a wasp, the man standing in front of him turned towards him, his face ruddy and his hat tipped back.

"Stop shovin' in, pal, watch yourself, eh?"

He was a drunkard of the argumentative school, the kind that gets up on its soap-box on a Sunday and bellows: "Up and at 'em, the bastards!"

"I'd like a coffee, please," the editor said to the girl behind the counter with exaggerated moderation. The drunk grabbed his sleeve.

"So I ain't worthy of an answer, am I?"

"Leave off, Charlie," his companion urged from the next table. "'E's a journalist; I just seen 'im come out of the newspaper offices. Best leave 'im alone or 'e'll name and shame you, and everybody'll believe it."

"Wait," Charlie was lurching. "I'll show him, he

ain't goin' to go shamin' 'onest folk who are just mindin' their own business!"

Mr Kotlach put the money for the coffee on the counter and left.

"Wait, I'm gonna give 'im what for," Charlie shouted from inside and suddenly shot out into the deserted street. The tails of his coat flapped around his drooping knees and his arms dangled down like a chimpanzee's.

"So, 'ow's it gonna be, you shit," he said, grabbing Mr Kotlach by the shoulder and breathing fumes of cheap spirits in his face.

"Leave me alone," said Kotlach. "Get away from me."

He could feel his lip quivering above his upper incisors, like a dog's when its patience has been tried.

"Get away from me," he snarled at the figure before him, which was beginning to spin in dark circles. "If you'll take my advice, you'll go about your business, now!"

"Aaaargh!" howled Charlie. "So that's 'ow it is! You think, 'cos you're a hintellectual, you can go about 'arassin' people. You just wait, I'll show you 'ho's boss!"

The dark circles settled into a single large smudge.

"Cookie," Kotlach bellowed.

"Your wish?" the dwarf darted out of a nearby passageway, wielding his cudgel with both hands.

Mr Kotlach looked at the puffy features of the man in front of him, dodged sideways and turned his back on him.

"The one at my back," he garbled, "grab your cudgel, kill him!"

Cookie jumped for glee, waved his cudgel, then there was a dull thud. Something crunched and there was a metallic sound as something hit the edge of the pavement. Kotlach turned round.

The drunk was staggering, the back edge of his deformed hat jammed down almost to his collar, and he was looking about him in an idiotic manner. Then he pointed ahead of him.

"'E's got a tame devil," he howled desperately, and flapping his hands like a duck, he ran towards an approaching taxi.

Cookie was squatting down beside a tree and trying hopelessly to fit together the two halves of the rotten shaft of his cudgel.

"Forgive me, sir," he looked up at Kotlach in despair. "I must pop and get a different cudgel. If you wouldn't mind remembering which gentleman it was..."

Then he jumped up and, employing the sorry remnant of his cudgel as a lever, deftly opened a drain cover.

"Listen, Cookie!"

"Yes, sir?"

"Don't bother. But if you would be kind enough to bring me a length of wire instead, about a metre long. I'll be waiting for you at home."

"At your service, sir," Cookie said, not fully understanding, and lowered his booted legs down into the drain. "But forgive me, I can't do it with wire!"

"Of course, Cookie," said Mr Kotlach.

After the drain cover clunked back into place, he sat down on the edge of the pavement and with his hands on his knees burst into tears in a way he hadn't since he was nine. He sniffed and snuffled and the tears rolled down his fat cheeks in a torrent.

He wasn't crying because Cookie had let him down, and he wasn't even crying because he had had such an awful day.

TRANSLATOR'S NOTE: KAREL MICHAL –
A WRITER OF THE CZECH 1960S.

I welcomed the opportunity to translate with open arms, remembering well the enthusiasm with which I, and thousands of ordinary Czech citizens, had bought and read it in 1967, when Spooks, *originally published in 1961, reappeared alongside Michal's new novella* Gypsová dáma *(Plaster Woman) and the previously published historical novella* Čest a sláva *(The Honour and the Glory, first published 1966). The book was refreshingly funny and the general reader, inevitably politicised to a greater or lesser degree, as was much of the public Central and Eastern Europe under Communism, relished the mysterious aura that accompanied many works of the incipient political Thaw which were either genuinely original (in the climate of a literature largely controlled from the political centre) or daring (by managing to slip through the censor's net and/or reflecting critically the often bizarre, regimented milieu out of which they came). In 1961* Spooks *had both these characteristics; by 1967 it could rely on both this reputation and the author's association with* Literární noviny, *the (then) fairly 'progressive' mouthpiece of the Union of Writers. It was a book that was queued for on publication day.*

Karel Michal was born Pavel Buksa in Prague in 1932. Everyday Spooks *was his first published work, after which he became a professional writer, with ancillary posts as a publisher's reader, filmscript editor and editor of* Literární noviny *(from 1966). In 1968, following the Soviet occupation of Czechoslovakia, he, like many other writers and artists, left his homeland for self-imposed exile in Switzerland. He died in Basle in 1984, survived by his wife, the poet Viola Fischerová (b. 1935), who returned to Prague after the 'Velvet Revolution' of 1989.*

Besides the works already mentioned, Michal is the author of a mildly quirky detective story, Krok stranou *(One step sideways, 1961) and a translation and adaptation of Congreve's The Way of the World* (Tak to na tom světě chodí, *1967, when it was also performed). In exile his main work was a collection of melancholy prose pieces,* Rodný kraj *(Homeland, 1977).*

Michal's impact on Czech literature has been slight, but the present book has made its mark in other ways, notably through the adaptation, by Michal himself or others, of several of the stories as films.

Although the book, if seen merely as grotesque fairy-tales for adults, is essentially timeless, scattered references, skilfully wo-

ven in to the narrative, point to the contemporary actions and prejudices of the powers-that-be or the public that had to live with them. Some comments are little more than generally applicable aphoristic platitudes, such as that 'there are certain principles that any decent individual holds sacred', that 'anyone who shows too much surprise merely betrays a lack of experience', or that 'people are not judged by what they do well, since that's their job, but by the mistakes they make'. More telling for the time and place were the jibes at the law and the corruption of doctors, or the description of 'experts', who 'go on in [their] discerning, tedious way about how things should be done, not how they [are]'; perhaps most telling for the time and place is the inference that all manner of persons could hold posts for which they were ill-qualified, exemplified by a confectioner in the role of chief engineer of public works. Michal cannot be said to have overdone the 'political sub-text' in this book, but in saying what he does, he is observing another of his aphorisms, that 'If people were afraid to say what they see, there'd be no point to anything'.

One final note: An early problem in translating this book was to find appropriate names for certain of the characters. With Pimpl, whose original name was Pupenec, I opted for a name that conveyed one of the senses of pupenec, *viz 'spot,*

pimple', but in a spelling that hinted at the alien environment.
Doodledor merely combines the first two syllables of doodle-
bug, *to hint at the 'bug-like' quality of the beast, and the 'dor'*
of dormer *to make the association with its preferred point of*
egress; that last syllable picks up on the creature's Czech name,
vikýřník. *Cookie sought to combine the acoustics of the original*
name, Kokeš, *with the 'slightly batty, cuckoo' sense of* cookie.
The big problem was plivník, *the original of what became*
Cockabogey. *In Czech this is an entire species of supernatu-*
ral creatures, as much as trolls or bogles in other folklores;
everyone knows what a plivník *is. The illustrations and the*
narrative together offer a clear enough image of what one is like,
so I just needed to combine the ideas that this is (a) unnatural,
and (b) male; the final form selected was modelled consciously
on chickabiddy *as its near-antithesis. I offer these solutions,*
along with the rest of the translation, to the reader in the hope of
his or her indulgence.

David Short   Windsor, April 2008

CONTENTS

EVERYDAY SPOOKS
KAREL MICHAL

English translation by David Short
Illustrations by Dagmar Hamsíková
Layout by Zdeněk Ziegler

Published by Charles University
in Prague, Karolinum Press
Ovocný trh 3–5, 116 36 Praha 1
http://cupress.cuni.cz
Prague 2008
Vice-rector-editor
Prof. PhDr. Mojmír Horyna
Edited by Martin Janeček
Typeset by MU studio
Printed by PB tisk, Příbram
First English edition

ISBN 978-80-246-1494-6